"I want sex," Sarah blurted into the receiver

Houston sat upright in bed. When he'd come back into town, he'd anticipated picking up where he and Sarah had left off—spending his nights burning up the sheets with her. Unfortunately, she hadn't been of the same mind. Until now.

"You want to have sex," Houston said, just to make sure he'd heard her correctly and this wasn't just an extension of the very erotic dream he'd been having.

"Not plain old sex. I want it in a shower, a movie theater, a public rest room and an elevator. It's unfinished business. Once we finish, things will get back to normal." He could hear in her voice that she felt the same heat he did, burning her up from the inside out.

"Which means we should get started right away." His body throbbed at the prospect.

"We'll start tomorrow."

Tomorrow? There was no way Houston would make it through another hour without her, much less an entire night. He wanted her and she wanted him, and they'd both admitted as much.

As far as he was concerned, there was no better time than the present.

Dear Reader,

It's hot this time of year in Texas, but it's *blazing* in the pages of my newest novel, *The Fantasy Factor,* thanks to Houston Jericho, the last of the notorious Jericho brothers.

Houston is a pro rodeo bull rider at the top of his game. But even more, he's a bad boy and proud of it! He isn't the least bit interested in changing his ways and settling down. He likes fast times and even faster women. When he rolls back into his hometown for the wedding of an old friend, the last thing he expects is to fall hard and fast for a good girl like Sarah Buchanan.

The thing is, Sarah isn't as good as she pretends to be. There's a bad girl lurking beneath the conservative clothes and quiet demeanor. One that refuses to forget Houston and the hot, sexy bargain they'd made when they were younger. Houston is more than ready to pick up where they'd left off, but Sarah isn't so eager. She's spent twelve years building a wholesome image and she isn't about to ruin it now.

The problem? She can't stop thinking about him, fantasizing about him, *wanting* him. She quickly realizes that the only way to maintain her good-girl status is to unleash the wild woman inside of her, temporarily of course, and finish what they'd started so long ago. She's looking for really great sex and closure, but what she finds is *really* great sex and a love strong enough to tame even the baddest bad boy!

I hope you enjoy Houston and Sarah's story! Drop me a line and let me know what you think. You can write to me c/o Harlequin Books, 225 Duncan Mill Road, Don Mills, Ontario M3B 3K9, Canada. Or visit me online at www.kimberlyraye.com or at www.gotsexauthors.com.

Happy reading!

Kimberly Raye

THE FANTASY FACTOR

Kimberly Raye

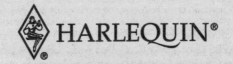

HARLEQUIN®

TORONTO • NEW YORK • LONDON
AMSTERDAM • PARIS • SYDNEY • HAMBURG
STOCKHOLM • ATHENS • TOKYO • MILAN • MADRID
PRAGUE • WARSAW • BUDAPEST • AUCKLAND

For my best buds,
Debbie Villanueva, Angela Fitch & Christine Kos.
Y'all are the greatest friends a girl could ask for!

ISBN 0-373-79135-6

THE FANTASY FACTOR

Copyright © 2004 by Kimberly Groff.

All rights reserved. Except for use in any review, the reproduction or
utilization of this work in whole or in part in any form by any electronic,
mechanical or other means, now known or hereafter invented, including
xerography, photocopying and recording, or in any information storage
or retrieval system, is forbidden without the written permission of the
publisher, Harlequin Enterprises Limited, 225 Duncan Mill Road,
Don Mills, Ontario, Canada M3B 3K9.

All characters in this book have no existence outside the imagination of
the author and have no relation whatsoever to anyone bearing the same
name or names. They are not even distantly inspired by any individual
known or unknown to the author, and all incidents are pure invention.

This edition published by arrangement with Harlequin Books S.A.

® and TM are trademarks of the publisher. Trademarks indicated with
® are registered in the United States Patent and Trademark Office, the
Canadian Trade Marks Office and in other countries.

www.eHarlequin.com

Printed in U.S.A.

1

SHE NEEDED A REALLY GOOD orgasm in a really bad way.

That was the only reason Sarah Buchanan kept stealing glances at the hot, handsome, sexy-as-sin cowboy standing at the bar of Cadillac's most notorious honky-tonk. Otherwise, she would have kept her gaze to herself and her attention fixed on the five women seated at the table with her.

She smiled and busied herself taking a drink of the Diet Coke she'd ordered. The cool liquid slid down her throat, but it did nothing to ease her pounding heart or the craving in the pit of her stomach. Her gaze slid sideways again, seeking out the western shirt and Wranglers. There.

Her gaze lifted, drinking in the sight of him, from the straw Resistol perched on top of his short-cropped blond head, down over the western shirt that outlined his broad, powerful shoulders, the large rodeo belt buckle that glittered at his trim waist, the tight jeans that cupped his crotch and hugged his powerful thighs, to the tips of his worn brown cowboy boots.

Houston Jericho was hot and hunky and he practically guaranteed a top-notch, first-class, screaming-good orgasm.

She knew that firsthand because she'd been on the receiving end, not once but three times. Three hot, wild, wicked times.

Of course, that had been a long time ago, and Sarah had since traded hot, wild and wicked for lukewarm, tame and boring. She'd given up her bad-girl tendencies—along with her sexy clothes and her favorite red leather cowboy boots—and completely changed her image.

Houston, however, looked as hot and wild and wicked as ever, his sensual lips crooked in a grin, his stance easy and relaxed and so damned sexy.

She got the distinct impression that he'd only gotten better with age.

"...your turn." The female voice drew her attention and she forced her gaze to the blonde who sat across the table from her. Janice Alcott was a corporate oil executive from Houston, and had, at one time, been the vice president of the Chem Gems, the only academic club at Cadillac High, a school where football and cheerleading had been considered hot and everything else—particularly anything that involved a textbook—not. "Looks like Maddie—" she

pointed to the blonde sitting next to her, their once-
upon-a-time president who'd traded her frumpy high
school image and shy demeanor for a svelte new figure and a tight leather halter top ''—isn't going to
nail this one. That means you only need five points
to beat her.''

They were on the last round of Who's the Baddest
Babe?—the sexy board game that had been the center of tonight's bachelorette party honoring Cheryl
Louise, the youngest Chem Gem, who was tying the
knot first thing tomorrow.

Cheryl had been a member of the club via her
older sister, Sharon, who'd been the smartest girl in
school and the founder of their group. She'd also
been one of Sarah's closest friends.

Until Sharon had wrapped her car around a telephone pole a few days before graduation. Maddie
had been in the driver's seat, and she'd walked away
with only a few scratches, thanks to the steering
wheel. She'd been lucky.

As lucky as Sarah herself, who would most certainly have been crammed into the passenger seat
with Sharon when the dashboard had caved in—had
her grandmother not grounded her yet *again,* and
sentenced her to her room for the weekend.

*''Child, why can't you be more like your mother?
She was always such a sweet girl. Always thinking
of others and making straight A's and doing me*

proud. Why, you wouldn't catch her swiping the school mascot the night before a football game. She always used her head.''

Because Lorraine Foster Buchanan had not only been the smartest girl in her class, she'd also been perfect. She'd always said the right things and worn the right clothes and married the right man and made all the right decisions....

Unlike her only offspring, who'd never managed to measure up. At least in Willemina Foster's eyes, and so Sarah had stopped trying early on. In fact, she'd gone the opposite direction, determined to set herself apart from her mother. To be different. To be her own person rather than a replacement for the daughter her grandmother had lost.

Instead of being sweet and wholesome, she'd been a daring, do anything rebel in red-hot cowboy boots who'd loved to shake things up and shock the fine, upstanding citizens of her small hometown. She'd been the first out of her clothes to go skinny-dipping down at Cadillac Creek, the first out of the car to toilet-paper the captain of the football team's house the night before homecoming, the first to ask a guy out for their junior prom, and the first to proposition Houston Jericho, the town's resident badass and the hottest, hunkiest guy ever to walk the hallowed halls of Cadillac High School.

Her gaze started to slide his way, but a passing waitress killed her line of vision. Thankfully.

She was here with her friends, *for* her friends. This was the first time they'd all been together in twelve years. And possibly the last they would be, since they led separate lives, two of them far, far away from Cadillac. She shouldn't waste her time scoping out men.

She gave herself a mental shake and forced her attention back to the game.

Maddie, despite her leather halter top and go-get-'em attitude, had just failed the latest assignment that would have made her an extra fifty points and secured the title. All of the other women were too far behind to win, but Sarah was right on her heels, and if she aced the next question, she would walk away the winner.

Not that Sarah intended to win, no matter how much she wanted to. She had an image to maintain. A wholesome, respectable, safe image that she'd spent too many years building to blow now.

"Girl, if you ace this, you'll be sleeping late tomorrow instead of picking up Uncle Spur," Eileen, the petite blond supermom told her.

Image aside, Sarah was in no hurry to spend two hours cooped up in a vehicle with Cheryl's uncle Spur, an ornery eighty-four-year-old man who prided himself on his tobacco spitting abilities and always being right.

She reached out, picked the top card from the deck and read it out loud.

"A true bad girl loves to make the first move,
Whether it's a kiss, a touch, or catching her groove.
So prove yourself by taking this chance,
Find a sinful minded man and ask him to dance!"

"That's no fair," Maddie complained. "I had to dance with someone *and* kiss him. All she has to do is dance."

"With a sinful minded man," Brenda pointed out, "which means he'll have more on his mind than, like, dancing if he's really in the sinful category. Not to mention, they're playing a slow song right now." A slow, sweet Toby Keith song wailed from the speakers.

"It's still no big deal," Maddie said. "This is too easy."

Maybe for any of the other five women at the table. But for Sarah, a former bad girl trying desperately to be good, dancing meant getting close, and slow-dancing meant getting even closer, and that meant trouble.

Her nipples throbbed at the thought, and frustration made her fingers tighten.

Yep, she needed a sinful man, all right. But needing and having were two very different things. She needed a lot of things. A new haircut. An extra large bag of Doritos. A pair of short-shorts and a slinky tank top to keep her cool while she worked at the family garden center she'd taken over from her grandmother several years back.

But she wasn't having any of those things because Sarah steered clear of anything and everything that spelled B-A-D, from junk food to revealing clothes to her favorite red boots to men. Life was short enough on its own without tempting fate by living dangerously.

She'd realized her mortality and decided to play it safe. At least that's what she wanted everyone to think, especially her grandma Willie. She owed the woman for saving her life that night, and so she followed a strict diet regime, got plenty of sleep, wore tasteful, conservative clothes and steered clear of sinful minded men.

Men who made a woman's heart pound and her legs quiver and her panties damp.

Men like Houston Jericho.

Her gaze shifted to him again and her lungs constricted. He was still as handsome as she remembered. More so because his wild, carefree aura now contained an air of maturity that plainly said he knew what to do, when to do it and exactly how to do it.

Definitely bad.

"Fifty points," Brenda Chance said. Brenda was a hopeless romantic. She'd married her high school sweetheart, Cal, given him a handful of kids and now lived and breathed the local PTA. "If you pull this off," she told Sarah, "you'll get, like, fifty points. More than enough to put you in the lead and win the game."

"I say she should pick another card," Maddie said. "Dancing is nothing for Sarah. I say she needs something more challenging. Something befitting the baddest bad girl ever to flash her boobs at a bus full of rival football players after a game."

Janice smiled. "Girlfriend, that was so funny."

Cheryl Louise grinned. "It was classic."

Sarah frowned. "It was stupid. It was forty below out. I nearly gave myself frostbite." She would have, except that she'd been laughing so hard, her heart pumping even harder, thanks to the rush of excitement at acting on a dare, that she'd actually felt warm. Hot.

Almost as hot as she felt right now.

She took a sip of her cold drink and forced a nice, easy, controlled breath. It was all about control. Something she'd manage to perfect thanks to twelve years of deprivation.

"I agree with Maddie," Janice said. "Sarah needs something more challenging. Girlfriend, she's already a bad girl, so that gives her an advantage over Maddie."

"Nonsense," Brenda said to Janice. "You and Maddie, like, have obviously been away too long. Sarah is the activities chairwoman for the local chamber of commerce. She spends her weekends hosting bake sales and organizing car washes. Why, she's about as bad as Pastor Standley's grandmother."

"She's still alive?"

"Barely. She's ninety-seven and she spends twenty-four/seven watching *Wheel of Fortune* reruns and reading *Reader's Digest*."

"Sounds totally *un*exciting," Janice said.

"That's Sarah," Brenda replied.

"Unexciting is good." Sarah took another sip of cola. "Too much excitement leads to stress and heart attacks."

Janice shook her head. "Whatever happened to the old Sarah we knew and loved and envied?"

But they all knew what had happened. They'd lost one of their closest and dearest friends the night before their high school graduation, and it had changed all of their lives forever.

Maddie, who'd been so set on following in her father's footsteps at the town's bake shop, had left to attend college in Dallas and ended up in a high-powered career with a leading cosmetics company. Janice had traded a local junior college for a major university and a career with a big oil company in Houston. Eileen had forfeited college to be a wife and mom and the local PTA president. Likewise, Brenda had given up college entirely to marry her high school sweetheart and have the first of five children, all of whom were scary at best—at least to Sarah, who'd grown up an only child with her grandmother and a house full of plants.

Cheryl Louise had still been in high school. She'd worked afternoons at the local five-and-dime and fantasized about Prince Charming sweeping in and saving her from her humdrum existence.

He'd swept in. Literally. Jack Beckham owned the only floor cleaning company in town and he'd been polishing the tile at the local TG&Y when he'd first spotted Cheryl Louise. He'd smiled and she'd smiled and now, several years later, they were about to say, "I do."

And Sarah?

She'd traded her big-city dreams, a chance at an architectural degree from the University of Texas and her one opportunity to get the hell out of her stifling hometown to stay right here, attend the local junior college, take over the family business and play the dutiful granddaughter.

"The card said 'sinful,' so don't even think about Marty Snifferdoodle." Janice pointed to the man sitting at the far end of the bar. He had a can of soda in one hand and a handful of peanuts in the other. He tipped his head back and tossed a peanut into the air, catching it in his mouth.

"He's coordinated," Sarah pointed out.

"Coordinated is not sinful."

"And don't think about old man Wally, either." Maddie eyed the ancient-looking man standing at the far end of the bar. His shock of white hair had been slicked to the side. He wore a starched shirt and Wranglers and made kissy faces every time a woman walked within his line of vision.

"He's sweet."

"He's old and frisky."

"But old, frisky men are sort of cute."

"Then you won't mind picking up Uncle Spur tomorrow," Maddie told Sarah.

Just the mention of Cheryl's obnoxious uncle made Sarah's stomach knot, and she pushed to her feet. Spur Tucker wasn't just obnoxious and loud-mouthed and downright mean. He was a threat to her nice, wholesome image.

If she had to hear him say even once more that her hair was too red or her skin too pale or her hips too wide or her butt too *out there,* she was liable to do what every woman in town had wanted to do since he'd started spending his holidays in Cadillac and running his mouth off—she was liable to wring his scrawny little neck until his eyes popped out.

Popping out an old man's eyes, even a hateful, ornery, critical old man's eyes, wasn't something a nice girl would do.

Which meant Sarah had to dance with Houston Jericho.

Just a dance, mind you. An innocent, you-stay-on-your-side-of-the-invisible-line-and-I'll-stay-on-mine sway of bodies.

No kissing him or jumping his bones or begging him to take her right here and now and sate her deprived libido.

No matter how hot he looked.

HE WAS TOO DAMNED HOT.

Houston tugged at the top button on his shirt and tossed down another swallow of his beer. Neither did much to cool the heat burning him up from the inside out. A heat that had very little to do with the crowded atmosphere of his old haunt and everything to do with the fact that *she* was here.

He still couldn't believe it. He'd been home a time or two over the years, but he'd never run into her. They kept company with totally different crowds now. While they'd both been into fast and furious fun way back when, Sarah Buchanan had since changed her ways. She spent her Saturday nights hibernating at home while he burned up the dance floors when he wasn't riding a thousand pound bull on the pro-rodeo circuit.

At least that's what Houston had heard about her.

He still couldn't believe it.

His gaze shifted across the room, to the table filled with familiar faces. Her nerdy friends, or so they'd been in high school. Age and success had turned them into a fairly nice-looking group.

Back then Sarah had fit in with them when it came to brains. As for her body... She'd been centerfold material, with a beautiful face, long hair, luscious breasts, a round, soft bottom and long legs.

Despite the talk around town, he didn't think she'd changed much at all. She still had a killer body, though it looked as if she tried to hide it. She wore a white, long-sleeved blouse with tiny pearl buttons rather than a tight T-shirt or sweater. Slacks rather than snug, fitted jeans. Conservative pumps rather than the come-and-get-me red cowboy boots she'd flaunted along with a lot of attitude.

She was still as hot as ever.

And she wasn't there.

He blinked and eyed the familiar four faces. Four, not five. Christ, he could have sworn he'd seen her just a few seconds ago.

Then again, maybe it had been wishful thinking.

An extension of any one of the fantasies that had haunted him over the past years. Sarah, naked and beautiful, in the shower. Sarah, naked and beautiful, in a public rest room. Sarah, naked and beautiful, in a dark movie theater. Sarah, naked and beautiful and riding him, in a moving elevator. Sarah, naked and beautiful, in any and all of the last four of *The Fantasy Factor: Sexiest Seven Places to Do It,* a self-help sex video that had caused quite a stir back in his high school days.

By today's standards, the content seemed extremely tame. There were no below-the-waist shots, though the video had hinted at total nudity. It had been primarily an instruction video for couples who wanted to spice up their sex life. But to a bunch of giggling teens in a small town, it had been a veritable porn fest.

The bootleg copy, courtesy of one of the football players who'd found the original in his parents' bedroom, had circulated throughout the senior class. It had been passed from one hand to another until a teacher had confiscated it from someone's locker.

By then, however, practically everyone had seen it, including Houston.

He'd caught his glimpse of it at an after-game party, the crowd made up primarily of seniors and a handful of freshman from nearby Kendall County Junior College. Sarah had been there, too, caught in a groping session with some junior college jerk who'd been pushing her too far, way too fast.

Houston had stumbled upon them in one of the back bedrooms when he'd been looking for the bathroom. They hadn't made it past second base, but the guy was quickly gunning for third despite Sarah's struggles. Houston could still remember the fear in her eyes and the relief when she'd caught a glimpse of him standing in the doorway. He'd pulled the guy off her, tossed him on his ass, and then he'd offered her his jacket to cover her torn blouse.

She'd taken his hand and, together, they'd slipped out the back door and headed for his souped-up Corvette. She hadn't wanted to go home for fear of facing her grandmother while she was still so shaken up, nor had she wanted to go back to the party and face her friends. She'd been fearful that the jerk would run his mouth and blow her hot-to-trot image. And so they'd wound up down by the creek with a bottle of homemade strawberry wine, an ice chest and some 7UP. They'd poured the wine and soda into the chest and mixed up some homemade wine coolers. Then they'd sat on the hood of his car and talked for the rest of the night until the sun had come up.

She'd admitted the truth to him then. Despite her ready, willing and able image when it came to sex, she was really only two out of three. She'd had only two sexual encounters and neither had been nearly as wonderful as she'd anticipated because they'd both been with assholes like the Junior College Jerk.

She wanted great sex. Wild sex. Hot sex. The stuff fantasies were made of.

She wanted Houston.

Even then, he'd had a reputation for being outstanding in the sack, and so she'd asked him to help her beef up her sexual knowledge by playing out the Sexiest Seven from the video.

He'd been a little shocked at her request, and a lot turned on because, like every other guy in school, he'd thought about being with her. Pleasuring her. Making her feel so good that she'd scream his name and come apart in his arms.

He'd kissed her then and they'd started that very night.

He'd expected it to be good. Sex was always good. But with Sarah, it had been phenomenal. She was so uninhibited when it came to her body, so vocal when it came to her feelings, and the combination had turned him on in a major way. Every time he'd touched her, kissed her, plunged into her, he'd seen the pleasure in her eyes and on her face, and he'd heard it in her loud, frantic cries.

Unlike most other girls, who'd been more interested in having him as a boyfriend than a lover, she hadn't been into playing games. She hadn't worried about saying the right things or holding out or maintaining an air of propriety. She'd been straightforward and free and very, very improper.

And he'd enjoyed every moment.

But then Sharon had passed away and Sarah had withdrawn and Houston had done what he'd been planning to do for as long as he could remember—he'd left his desperately small town and his sorry excuse for a father, and he'd built his name and his reputation as one of the best bull riders on the pro-rodeo circuit.

Houston was the middle brother of the notorious Jericho brothers. Austin was the oldest. Dallas the youngest. All had been as bad as a hot summer day was long. They'd been the town's rebels, a legacy inherited from their hell-raising father and wild-child mother. His mother had died early on, just months after giving birth to Dallas. She'd been diabetic and the birth had been too much for her. There'd been complications and her kidneys had failed. She'd fought for her life on a dialysis machine, but it hadn't been enough to save her. She'd passed on, and his father had crawled into a bottle and the three boys had been left to fend for themselves.

They'd all grown up to be independent, none of them depending on anyone except one another to overcome their past and rise above the town's expectations of them. Dallas had built a successful construction company. Austin was a rancher with the fastest growing spread in the county. And Houston was this close to breaking the national bull riding record of ten consecutive championships.

He'd worked hard to get to this point. Over the years, he'd spent most of his time on the road, focused on the next practice and the next competition. Always focused.

Except at night, when the exhaustion weighing on his muscles wasn't enough to pull him into a decent sleep. Then he would close his eyes and sometimes—oftentimes—picture Sarah.

They'd made it through the first three of the Sexiest Seven. They'd gotten hot and heavy on the bank of Cadillac Creek on a moonlit night, which had satisfied number one—sex outside in nature. They'd done the wild thing in her Grandma's Impala, which had satisfied number two—sex in the back seat of a car. They'd set each other on fire in a cheap but clean room at Hotel Heaven just outside the county line, checking off number three—sex in a sleazy motel room. They'd been scheduled to fulfill number four—getting slippery and wet in the shower—when one of Sarah's best friends had passed away.

Sarah had changed then and he'd left, and they'd never made it into the shower for number four of the Sexiest Seven, or into a crowded movie theater for number five, or a public rest room for number six, or an elevator for number seven.

No, they'd never had a chance to finish, but he'd often thought about it. Fantasized about it.

"...there, sugar?" The voice drew his attention and he turned to see the sultry blonde to his right who had been coming on to him all night. He'd been trying to warm up to what she'd been offering, but then Sarah had walked into the bar and the blonde had suddenly lost all her appeal. Now she licked her lips suggestively. "This place is getting too crowded. What do you say we cut out of here and have a little private party of our own?"

"I'd love to, honey, but I think I'd better stick around a little while longer." He eyed the group of men at the bar, all arms raised in a toast to the groom, who wore a foam ball and chain around his neck. "Jack and I go way back."

What the hell was he saying?

He *wanted* to get out of here. Out of the building, out of his clothes, away from the damned heat. He needed to sate the lust burning him up from the inside out.

Unfortunately, the lust had nothing to do with this woman and everything to do with the woman he'd spotted only a few minutes ago.

Correction—the woman he'd imagined only a few minutes ago.

"Then how's about an itty-bitty dance?" the blonde asked. She moved her hips suggestively, rubbing her pelvis against his thigh. "I bet I can change your mind about the private party."

He tugged at his collar and tipped back his Resistol. "Maybe later. I think I need another beer." She glared and walked off while he stepped up to the bar and signaled the bartender.

A minute later, he slid a few dollars across the bar top and raised an ice-cold mug to his lips. The freezing liquid slid down his throat in a rush of cool relief. He grimaced. While the beer hit the spot, he didn't have much of a taste for it after watching his old man drink himself to death. Which was why he never passed his three beer maximum when he drank.

If he drank.

But tonight was a special occasion. One of his old buddies was tying the knot tomorrow and so Houston had come back to Cadillac. Only for a few days, then he was off to practice for the next Pro Bull Riding championship in three weeks. Before then, however, he was going to make another pass through town to say goodbye to Miss Marshalyn Simmons, the most headstrong woman ever to come after him with a switch and a good lecture. The whole town was scheduled to say goodbye to her at a party being planned in her honor over at the VFW Hall.

She was moving down to Florida to live with her sister. Miss Marshalyn had grown tired of the hot and sticky climate. Tired of living alone. Tired, period. She wasn't getting any younger and the hassle and responsibility of caring for a three-hundred-acre spread and a fading farmhouse was simply too much for her.

She wanted peace of mind, and so she'd made Houston and his brother Austin—the two Jericho brothers still single from the original notorious three—a proposition they couldn't refuse.

Dallas, the youngest boy, had already found the love of his life and walked down the aisle. He was now only a few months away from becoming a father—a responsibility Houston knew Dallas would take very seriously thanks to their own sorry excuse for a father.

Miss Marshalyn wasn't the least worried about Dallas, which was why she'd already handed over a prime hundred acres to him as a present for the new baby.

It was Houston and Austin who caused her the most concern. She wanted them to trade in their bad-boy ways and settle down. In return, she promised one hundred acres to each of them. But only if they managed to convince her they'd really and truly changed their ways in time for her going-away party.

Houston slid a glance toward the exit door where his brother Austin had disappeared only a few minutes earlier after having danced with Maddie Hale, the shy, frumpy leader of the Chem Gems who'd turned into a bona fide hottie. Much too hot for Miss Marshalyn's tastes. She wanted both men to choose a prospect from the town's pick of nice, quiet, wholesome conservative good girls.

Maddie no longer qualified, and it was no wonder Austin—who was dead set on making Miss Marshalyn happy—had walked out before things had really heated up.

Houston, on the other hand, had no intention of taking Miss Marshalyn up on her offer. He wasn't the settling-down type. He'd worked too damned hard to get the hell out of Cadillac. He certainly wasn't coming back now. Not permanently. Not ever.

He'd meant to say as much to Miss Marshalyn. He'd tried, but she'd cut him off in that way that told him she knew best. And so he hadn't been able to set the record straight about the land and the fact that he was leaving.

He would, of course. He just didn't see the need to disappoint her right now. He had a good two weeks. Plenty of time to let her down slowly, easily, before he had to leave for Las Vegas and the Pro Bull Riding Finals, where he was scheduled to compete for his tenth consecutive championship.

A record-breaking win that would put him right up there with the greatest riders of all time.

The knowledge didn't send nearly the jolt of adrenaline through him that it usually did. Understandable, since he was still sore from a hard but high-scoring ride the night before in Cheyenne. A man most certainly couldn't be excited when it hurt just to breathe.

He drew a deep breath and an ache gripped his left lower rib cage. He hadn't broken any bones this time, but he'd come close. She'd almost stomped him square in the chest. She would have if he hadn't rolled just in time.

In time, but still too late. He was getting slower each and every time he hit the ground. No one else noticed, but he did. He felt the weariness pulling at his bones and it bothered him.

PBR champion cowboys weren't slow. Slowing down meant losing, and Houston had been winning much too long to stop now. Even more, he liked winning. He loved it. He lived for it.

He just wished it didn't hurt like hell.

"I hate to bother you." A soft, sweet voice drifted from behind him. "But would you care to dance?"

"I'm afraid not—" he started to say as he turned. The words stumbled to a halt in his throat when he found himself staring at the sultry redhead who'd lived and breathed in his memories for the past twelve years.

His pain faded into a rush of heat and his heart thundered because Sarah Buchanan wasn't a figment of his imagination this time.

She was real. With eyes as warm as the hot fudge he loved to pour on his favorite vanilla ice cream, and just as decadent. And she was standing so close he could actually touch her.

And that's just what he did.

2

HOUSTON JERICHO HAD TOUCHED his fair share of women. But none had ever felt as soft or as warm as Sarah Buchanan.

The notion struck him the moment he trailed his fingertips down the side of her face, under the curve of her jaw, down the smooth column of her throat, until the silky fabric of her collar stopped him.

"You're real."

"I...yes." She licked her bottom lip and he had the urge to lean down and catch the plump flesh between his teeth and nibble. "And, um, so are you. Not that I had a doubt. I mean, I saw you and I knew right away that it was you, even from a distance. But you look better up close. Bigger." His grin widened as she stumbled over her words.

A crazy thing, because Sarah Buchanan had never had trouble finding the right words for anything. She'd always said what was on her mind, in her thoughts. She didn't look for the right words the way she seemed to be doing right now.

His mind flashed back to the few times he'd been

home in the past to see his brothers. The visits had always been brief. Two days at most, just like this time. He'd always been in such a hurry that he'd never actually run into her. But he'd heard about her.

That she'd changed. That she'd outgrown her rebel attitude like a trendy pair of shoes. Yep, he'd heard the talk, but he'd never believed it.

He didn't believe it now, despite the cautious air about her and the way she seemed to stiffen when he smiled at her. There was just something about the way she looked at him with those deep brown eyes that said she was hungry for him.

As hungry as she'd been at seventeen. Maybe more so, considering that she was a full-grown woman now, with a woman's curves, a woman's maturity, a woman's needs.

"I care."

"I beg your pardon?"

"You asked me if I cared to dance. I do."

"Oh." A few seconds ticked by as reality seemed to register. "Oh."

He grinned and watched her stiffen again. "After you, honey." He let her lead him out onto the dance floor, through a sea of moving bodies, straight into the heart of things, which was just what he'd expected.

Sarah had always been the center of attention. Not because she'd wanted to be, simply because she attracted attention with her free spirit and her I-don't-give-a-shit attitude.

She bypassed the middle and kept moving until they'd reached the far side of the dance floor, where it wasn't so crowded or loud.

She put one hand on his shoulder and the other on his arm, as if she meant to keep some distance between them.

Right.

He pulled her close, plastering them together from chest to thigh, holding her securely with one arm tight around her waist.

"You're definitely real. And warm. And you smell just like those raspberries we used to pick out in old man Baxter's field."

Houston's words slid into her ears, coaxing her to soften in his arms the way the warm heat of his body urged her to relax and let her guard down.

She wanted to.

She'd been so good for so long, and the need to let her hair down and stop thinking, worrying, just once was nearly unbearable.

"That was a long time ago," she said, the words more for herself. But they did little good.

"What's wrong?"

"Not a thing."

"You're stiff."

"Stiff is good."

"I won't argue that with you," he said, and she became instantly aware of the hardness pressed against the soft cradle of her thighs. Heat flowered low in her belly, spreading through her body like a flame sweeping dry brush. "But the idea is usually for me to take care of the stiffness, while you soften up."

"I can't. I mean, I don't. I don't soften up anymore. Haven't you heard? I'm not like that anymore."

"I heard, but I didn't believe it."

"Why not?"

"Because it's pretty far out, don't you think? I mean, you, sexy Sarah, a prude? That's like saying Santa Claus is really the Easter Bunny. It's just not natural."

"It's true."

"Like hell. Santa wouldn't be caught dead hopping around in a furry white suit with big floppy ears and big floppy feet. Santa's way too cool. He's got the whole black biker boot thing going on." She saw the teasing light in his eyes and found herself back in the past, charmed by his smile and soothed by his teasing voice.

And for a split second, she actually forgot that things had changed. That she'd changed.

Her hands crept up the hard wall of his chest, her arms twined around his neck and she leaned closer.

His heart beat against her breasts. His warm breath sent shivers down the bare column of her neck. His hands splayed at the base of her spine, one urging her even closer while the other crept its way up, as if reacquainting itself with every bump and groove, until he reached her neck. A few deft movements of his fingers and the tight ponytail she wore unraveled and her hair spilled down her back. His hand cradled the base of her scalp, massaging for a few blissful moments, making her legs tremble.

For the next few moments, she forgot all about the game and her friends and the all-important fact that no self-respecting lady would be caught dead with Houston Jericho, much less pressed up against him on a crowded dance floor for everyone to see.

She tilted her head back and found him staring down at her. The past pulled her back, to a moonlit night when he'd looked at her just this way, as if he wanted to take slow, sweet bites and savor every inch of her.

He'd done just that and she had the sudden thought that she wanted him to do it again. Right here. Right now.

Don't do this, a voice whispered. *You can't do this.*

She was different now. At least, that's what she wanted everyone to think. And they weren't going to think any such thing if she lost her head right in the middle of the dance floor and pressed herself up against him. And rubbed this way and that. And touched him just so—

A loud whistle ripped through the air and shattered the seductive spell she'd been lost in. She jerked around to see Maddie, Eileen, Janice, Brenda and Cheryl Louise. They waved and gave a thumbs-up.

"What's that all about?"

"Just a game."

"What kind of game? To see who gives the loudest wolf whistle?"

"Actually, it's about dancing." She forced her fingers to let go of his collar and she pulled away. "And I just won. If you'll excuse me…" She didn't wait for a response. She darted away from him and left him staring after her.

His gaze drilled into her back, and it was all she could do to keep from turning and running back and begging him to take her to bed.

Or, more important, straight into a nice warm shower. Because that's what he did in her fantasies. What they'd planned on doing for their fourth encounter so long ago. What he'd never had the chance to do because she'd changed and he'd left and life had come between them.

She said a quick goodbye to her friends before heading for the rear exit. Out in the parking lot, she climbed behind the wheel of her car. As she shoved the key into the ignition, her arm bumped a giant cardboard box filled with vases for the centerpieces she was going to put together tonight for Cheryl Louise's reception tomorrow. Glass clinked and the engine groaned.

She gave one last look at the exit door, half expecting, half hoping that he would come after her. He didn't, and a swell of disappointment went through her, quickly followed by a wave of relief.

The last thing, the very *last* thing she needed in her life was to have Houston Jericho running after her. He wasn't her type and she wasn't his.

Even if he did suit her perfectly in her dreams.

This was real life, not some hot, erotic fantasy.

More important, this was her life now—her calm, conservative, boring life, and she wasn't about to spice it up and ruin her image by losing her head, or her hormones, over Houston Jericho.

It was all about keeping her perspective the next time she saw him.

If that didn't work, she would just have to keep her distance.

"MY, MY, BUT THAT WAS a beautiful ceremony." Miss Marshalyn sighed and finished penning her name in the guest book. "Marriage is such a blessed union," she told Houston as she wrapped an arm around his and started inside the VFW Hall for the reception. "Don't you think, dear?"

"For some, I'm sure it is. But for others—"

"Nonsense. It's blessed for everyone. Oh, look, there's Jennie Mayfield." She pointed to a petite blonde oohing and aahing over a small baby. "That's her new niece. She has nine of them, and seven nephews, and she dotes on them."

"Good for her."

"No, good for you. If she thrives on her nieces and nephews, she's sure to dote on her own children, and you most certainly want a wife who adores her children."

"I'm sure she'll make a great wife. Not for me, but for someone—"

"There's Darlene Davenport. She's the secretary over at the bingo hall. She knows everything about gardening."

"That's good."

"You're darned tootin' it is. A man deserves fresh vegetables with his dinner, and since you'll have one hundred acres of your very own, you can devote plenty of room to a nice garden."

"About the land—"

"No need to thank me, dear," she cut in, waving him silent.

"I wasn't going to thank you. I was going to tell you that I really can't—"

"Why, there's Margie Weston!" Miss Marshalyn blurted. "I haven't seen her in ages. I must go say hello. We'll chat later, dear." Before Houston could blink his eyes, he found himself standing alone. But not for long.

It seemed that the old woman wasn't just pointing out prospects to him. She seemed to be pointing him out to all of her prospects. In a matter of minutes, he found himself surrounded by a handful of women talking about everything from muddy diapers to various species of tomatoes.

"I like the cherry ones, myself, but they do require extra care to grow. What about you, Houston? What's your favorite tomato?"

"I don't eat tomatoes."

"How about cucumbers?"

"Never liked them."

"What about squash? I've never met a man who didn't like squash."

"Can't stand the stuff. Wow, there's Darcy Waters. I haven't seen her in ages." He tried Miss Marshalyn's avoidance tactic. "I have to say hello."

He left the group staring after him, muttering about what a loosey goosey Darcy Waters used to be.

They were right. She'd been loose back then, and she was still going strong, he quickly discovered after saying hello. Five husbands, an equal number of divorces and three kids later, she still found time to keep the dance floor hot over at Cherry Blossom Junction and every other honky-tonk in the surrounding counties. She liked astrology and Marlboro Lights and he quickly discovered that he didn't like her half as much as he liked Sarah Buchanan.

Even if Sarah was wearing a hideous orange bridesmaid's dress and doing her best to avoid him.

He shifted his gaze to the woman currently straightening the bride's lengthy train. She busied herself behind the scenes rather than out front the way he remembered.

She's different now, a voice whispered. Last night proved what everyone said about her—namely, that she kept a low profile, walked the straight and narrow and conducted herself like a bona fide lady. At the same time, he couldn't forget the wild light in her eyes when she'd stared up at him for those few moments on the dance floor, as if she'd wanted more from him than just a dance.

Maybe. And maybe it was just wishful thinking because *he* wanted more from *her* than just one dance.

He couldn't help but wonder if she tasted as good as he remembered, if she felt as soft, if she sounded just as breathless when he nibbled at her neck and stroked her nipples.

And Houston had never been a man just to sit

around and wonder about anything. He went after what he wanted and found out for himself.

He started toward her.

"I DON'T BITE." The smooth, silky voice came from behind, followed by a firm, familiar touch on her shoulder. "Except for that one time, but it was only because you wanted me to."

Sarah's hand faltered on the cup of punch she'd just poured. Raspberry sherbet mixed with ginger ale sloshed over the side and trickled over her fingers. She set the cup aside, next to the dozen or so others she'd poured in the past few minutes and did her best to calm her pounding heart.

Pounding, when she'd promised herself just last night that she wasn't going to get nervous. Or excited. Or turned on.

Especially turned on. She had a reputation to protect and salivating at the first sign of the town's hottest bad boy was not in keeping with her goody-goody image.

"Hello to you, too."

"I didn't walk clear across this room to say hello. I tried to do that more than two hours ago when I first arrived. But the minute I started toward you, you turned and bolted for the kitchen."

"I didn't bolt. I simply moved very swiftly. I had

to help arrange the vegetable trays before everyone arrived from the church.''

"That's what I told myself, so I waited a little while, until I saw you over by the cake table. I started toward you again, but you took off for the kitchen again."

"I forgot the fresh flower bouquets to decorate the groom's cake table."

"That's what I told myself, so I waited again until you finished setting up the flowers and I started over. I even called out and waved that time, too."

"Really? I didn't see you."

"I could have sworn you did, but then you headed off to the kitchen again."

"I had to get the bag of fresh rose petals to sprinkle on the bride's cake table."

"That's what I told myself, so I waited until you finished and then I started over again. I even called out that time."

"Really? I didn't hear a thing."

"I didn't think so. Otherwise you wouldn't have headed for the kitchen again."

"I had to help with the punch. The lady who was supposed to man the table came down with a bad stomach virus a half hour ago so here I am."

"And here I thought this was just another reason to avoid me."

"I'm not avoiding you. I'm simply busy." To illustrate her point, she reached for the ladle and served up another cup of punch. "Thirsty?"

"Actually, I'm hungry."

"There's everything from pigs-in-a-blanket to mini pizza rolls." But she knew by the look in his eyes that he wasn't talking about food. She tamped down on her own growling stomach and reached for another empty cup.

"The wedding is over." His hand closed over hers. He took the cup from her hand and set it to the side. "It's time to have some fun."

"I promised I would serve the punch."

"No one wants any punch. They're too busy dancing." He indicated the dance floor overflowing with couples two-stepping to an old George Strait tune. The only person who wasn't dancing was Wes Early, the town's only videographer. Cheryl Louise had hired him to record her wedding memories and he was currently walking from couple to couple, zooming in for close-ups and capturing good wishes and advice with his camcorder. "Let's dance."

"I can't. I mean, I don't want to. I promised my grandma Willie that I would keep her company."

His gaze followed hers to the old woman who sat at one of the large round tables. A half dozen other white-haired ladies surrounded her. A maze of dominoes covered the table.

"I don't think she needs you."

She stared at her grandmother. The old woman lifted her head, caught her granddaughter's gaze and smiled before turning her attention back to the game and her last domino—a double six—which she slid into the center of the table before letting loose a loud "I win!"

"That's her domino club. They get together every Saturday night. I guess they didn't see the wedding as an excuse to call off tonight's game."

"She looks happy."

"She is happy."

"And what about you? Are you happy?"

"I don't mind serving punch."

"That's not what I'm talking about. Are you happy here? In Cadillac?"

No. "Yes," she blurted. "I'm very happy. I've never been so happy. I've got my business and my grandma. Life is all right."

"All right?" He eyed her. "What happened to amazing? Awesome? Explosive?" He named off every adjective she'd ever used when talking about the future and the life that waited for her beyond the city limits.

"I'm not the same irresponsible girl I was back then."

"Because…"

Because she'd barely survived last night's close encounter. If she had to feel his arms around her again, or smell his intoxicating scent, or stare into his eyes, she wasn't so sure she could make it through with her cover still firmly in place. "Because I can't."

"Why?"

"Because it's late." She glanced at her watch, her brain scrambling for an excuse to step away from him. To run away before she did something really outlandish like throw her arms around him and kiss him right here and now with everyone looking on. "And I've got to get up early for work."

"Tomorrow's Sunday. The nursery is closed."

"But I'm still working. I've got a full greenhouse to inventory before my new deliveries on Monday. It'll take all day, so I have to get a very early start. Nice talking to you. If you'll excuse me—"

"Not this time." He caught her hand and tugged her after him, to the far side of the room and a small, private corner behind several large potted palms draped in white tulle and twinkling white lights.

"What are you doing?"

"Trying to figure out why you won't dance with me." He hauled her in front of him and backed her into the corner. "Other than the fact that it's late and you have to be up early. I know there's more to it, Belle."

Belle. As in Jezebel. "Nobody calls me that any-more."

"As I recall, no one else ever did. It was just me. I also recall that you liked me calling you that, almost as much as you liked dancing with me."

"Maybe I don't like to dance anymore."

"You liked it just fine last night."

"I wanted to win a game last night. I needed to dance with a hot guy to beat Maddie, and you were the only hot guy there." When he didn't look the least bit convinced, she added, "You were hot and I needed hot. It wasn't because I wanted to dance, certainly not that I wanted to dance with *you*. I didn't. Not last night, and not now."

"Is that so?"

"Look, things are different now. I'm different."

"Really?" He fingered the conservative neckline of the hideous orange bridesmaid's dress. "You mean your heart doesn't pound when I do this?"

She managed to shake her head despite that he could undoubtedly feel the frantic *thud thud* against the pad of his finger.

"And your blood doesn't rush when I do this?" He trailed his fingertip over the edge of the dress, over the material until he brushed her nipple through the fabric.

"Not at all."

"And you don't get even the slightest bit wet when I do this?" His touch swept south until she felt the press of his fingertip at the vee of her legs. He traced a little circle and heat fired low in her belly.

"I...don't."

"Why?"

"Because..." She licked her lips and tried to ignore the sensation sweeping along her nerve endings. It felt so good and he felt so good and she wanted nothing more than to close her eyes and simply *feel*. "This is a bad idea."

"Because you don't want me?" He leaned down, his warm breath brushing the sensitive shell of her ear. "Or because you do?"

"Because..." She tried to think of an explanation, but then her gaze caught his and she couldn't think. She could only feel. The warmth of his body so close to hers. The throb of her nipples. The tightening between her legs. The tingle of her lips. "I really want to kiss you," she blurted. And then she did.

He didn't seem the least bit surprised to feel her lips against his own. His mouth was wet and warm and welcoming.

He plunged his tongue deep, tangling with hers in a fierce kiss that made her thighs quiver and her nipples ache and her hormones chant *yes, yes, yes* while her brain screamed *no, no, no!* She tasted him, licking and exploring in a fast and furious rhythm that quickly calmed into something a little less frantic and a lot more dangerous.

But Sarah Buchanan didn't do fast or furious or dangerous, *especially* dangerous. Not anymore.

The truth echoed in her head, but it wasn't enough to make her stop. It was the voice that did that.

"Say something to the bride and groom."

Sarah pulled away to find a video camera trained on her.

Reality hit her as Wes Early grinned and said into the mini microphone attached to his camcorder, "Weddings aren't just about forming new relationships, folks. They're about renewing old ones, as well. Houston and Sarah were once the hottest couple in high school and it seems they're still heating things up—"

"Thanks for the suggestion," Sarah cut in, with the only excuse her frazzled brain could come up with. "I'll definitely give some thought to replacing the chamber's annual bake sale with a kissing booth."

"What?" Houston stared down at her, deep into her eyes, and her heart did a double thump.

"Your idea for the chamber of commerce to host a kissing booth instead of a bake sale. It's got potential but you didn't need to demonstrate."

"I didn't—" he started.

"Shame on me for getting caught up in the town's business on your special day," she cut in, fixing her gaze on the video camera and forcing a smile. "Congratulations and I wish you both the best.'' And then she darted under Houston's arm and left both men and a live camcorder staring after her.

A video camera, of all things. Not only had she blown the conservative image she'd managed to build for herself, she'd done it on tape for everyone to see.

She forced away the thought and headed out to the parking lot. She was already behind the wheel when she remembered that she hadn't even said goodbye to anyone. Not Cheryl Louise or her friends or her grandma Willie, who'd ridden over with some of the ladies from her domino group.

It was all Houston's fault. He was stirring the bad girl locked deep inside of her, coaxing out the old Sarah with his sinful smiles and naughty words and sexy heat.

If she wasn't careful, she was liable to blow the good girl cover she'd spent the past twelve years perfecting. A cover so convincing that she'd actually started to believe it herself, to accept it, to *like* it.

No, she didn't like the person she'd become any more than she liked this desperately small town. But this was the life she'd made for herself and so she had to live it.

For her grandmother's sake.

She closed her eyes, remembering the night of Sharon's death when Brenda had called, so tearful and frantic. While the news had devastated Sarah, it had nearly killed her grandmother.

The old woman had sat there, the phone pressed to her ear as she'd listened to Brenda's voice. Her gaze had been fixed on Sarah, the awful truth vivid in her eyes—it could have been Sarah who'd died that night. It would have been had she not grounded Sarah because she'd been late for her curfew the night before.

The realization had been too much for her grandmother. Her blood pressure had escalated and she'd had a mild heart attack.

Sarah could still see her grandmother's pale face, hear her frantic whisper.

"You have to take care, Sarah. You have to think. I can't lose you the way I lost your mother. My heart can't take it."

"Everything's going to be all right, Grandma. I promise. Things are going to be different. I'm going to be different. You don't have to worry about me anymore. You won't have to worry about me ever again."

Sarah had made the tearful promise in the ambulance en route to Tyler County Hospital as she'd held her grandmother's hand and prayed for the old woman's recovery. A promise she'd kept for the past twelve years. One she would continue to keep until her grandma Willie drew her last breath.

That meant steering clear of Houston Jericho while he was back in town. Out of sight, out of mind, as the saying went, and now that the wedding was over, he would surely head back out of town. While he'd come home a few times over the years, he rarely stayed more than a day or two because of his busy rodeo schedule and the fact that he hated being cooped up in this town as much as she had so long ago.

He would hit the road again. Probably tonight. At the very latest, first thing tomorrow.

Good riddance. The sooner he left, the sooner she could get back to her life and forget about tonight and the kiss and the fact that she'd almost blown it in front of everyone.

Almost, but not completely. She'd managed to explain it away to Wes, and if anyone happened to mention it again, she would merely blush and stammer and repeat the lame excuse. And that would be that.

She drew a deep breath.

Yes, the temptation was over. At least in reality.

When she closed her eyes later that night, however, he came to her in her dreams, kissing and touching and stirring her in the most erotic fantasy she'd had in a long, long time.

Just a fantasy, she reminded herself when she awoke with her heart pounding and her skin flushed and her body wet with wanting. It wasn't as if the man who'd reached for her, pleasured her, was real.

No, the real man was long gone from Cadillac, or he soon would be. And with any luck, he wouldn't ever come back.

3

HE WAS STILL IN TOWN.

Sarah discovered that the moment she walked out of her house early the next morning and headed down the walkway toward the three-thousand-square-foot greenhouse that housed the Green Machine.

Worse, he was here.

He'd traded in the old souped-up Corvette he'd driven back in high school for a brand-new gleaming black Chevy pickup truck—evidence that Houston Jericho was no longer the poorest kid in town. He'd made something of himself.

But then, she'd had no doubt that he would. He'd been so dead set on showing up his drunk of a father and proving to any and everyone that while he might look like his old man, he was nothing like him.

She glimpsed his handsome face through the window, his eyes trained on her, his lips set in a grim line. As if he was thinking real hard about some question and he wasn't too pleased with the answer.

As if he wasn't any more happy to be here than she was to see him here.

She pondered the notion for a few seconds as she unlocked the door latch and tried to pretend for all she was worth that his presence didn't affect her.

Fat chance.

Every nerve in her body was keenly aware of him. She felt his warm gaze on her profile and a slow heat swept over her, from the tips of her toes clear to the top of her head, until she all but burned in the early morning heat. She shifted her stance, her thighs pressing together, and an ache shot through her. Her nipples pebbled, rubbing against her bra as she tried to unlock the stubborn latch.

The more determined she became, the more the old piece of rusty steel fought back.

"Come on," she muttered. Her hands trembled and her heart slammed a furious rhythm against her rib cage. "I don't need this today." Not after the night she'd had. A sleepless, frustrated night that had her feeling nervous and anxious and dissatisfied. "I really don't need this."

"What *do* you need?"

The deep voice froze her hands as she realized that he was right here. Right now. Right behind her.

Worse, he leaned in, his arms coming around her on either side, his hands closing over hers to steady her.

"I, um, need to get this blasted thing open. It's stuck."

"Let's see what we can do about that." His large dark hands were a stark contrast against her pale white fingers. His warm palms cradled the tops of her hands. The rough pads of his fingertips rasped against her soft flesh and heat spiraled through her body.

Her grip tightened on the key.

"Easy, now." His voice rumbled over her bare shoulder and warm breath brushed her skin. Goose bumps chased up and down her arms and she came *this* close to leaning back into him, closing her eyes and enjoying the delicious sensation. Just for a little while.

She stiffened and fought for her precious control. Twelve years of cloaking herself in it should have made it easy to find, but not with Houston so close. Too close for her to breathe, much less think, much less pretend.

"I don't think it's the lock that's giving you trouble as much as the way you're approaching the matter. You really need to loosen up." As he said the words, she got the distinct impression that he was talking about more than just her grip on the key.

"Thanks for the advice, but no thanks. I do not need to loosen up." To prove her point, she focused every ounce of energy she had on ignoring the delicious feelings assaulting her body. She held her breath and turned the key and tried to ignore the fingers that burned into her and guided her a little to the left and then a little to the right and... *click.*

His arms fell away as she unhooked the padlock and tried to calm her thundering heart.

"What are you doing here?" she demanded as she turned on him. She busied her lips with the tightest frown she could manage, considering she wanted to kiss him more than she wanted her next breath.

"Inventory. You said you were starting early, so I thought I'd stop by and give you a hand."

"I mean here. In town. I thought you were leaving."

"I was. I am. But Miss Marshalyn's party is in two weeks and I'd planned on coming back for that before heading off to Vegas for the PBR finals. It didn't make much sense to make a second trip here when the only thing on my schedule for the next two weeks is practice. I can hang around and do that right here instead of going back and forth."

It made sense, and it also made her heart give a double thump. *Two weeks.* She'd barely made it through last night. How ever was she going to endure two solid weeks knowing he was right here in town, a phone call away?

"You look awful pale. Is everything all right?"

"I'm tired," she muttered.

"You sure about that? Because, for a second there, I could have sworn you were going to kiss me."

"Trust me, I'm not going to kiss you."

"You kissed me last night."

"That was temporary insanity. I was tired because of the wedding and I wasn't thinking. If I had been, I would never have kissed you. I don't do that anymore. I'm different now."

"Maybe." He shrugged. "Maybe not."

"What's that supposed to mean?"

"That *maybe* you just want me to think that you're different, the way you want everyone else to think that. But I know better. I know you."

"You did. A long time ago."

"I still do. You kissed me because you wanted me." His gaze darkened. "You still taste as good as you did way back when."

"I really have a lot of work to do." She grabbed her clipboard.

"Where should I start?"

"You don't have to help me."

"I want to." His gaze told her he wanted a lot more, but he was backing off, giving her some space to come to terms with what she was feeling. As if she could.

Coming to terms involved acknowledging her feelings and deciding on a course of action. And action, as far as Houston Jericho was concerned, was completely out of the question.

"You start on that end. All the plants are labeled. Simply write the name down and do a count for each one. There's another clipboard behind the counter."

She turned and wound her way to the far side, putting as much distance as possible between them. She needed some distance.

From the past.

From the present.

From *him*.

If he wasn't so close, then he wouldn't be so tempting, and maybe, just maybe, she could make it through the rest of the day without another fall from grace.

With that in mind, she put every ounce of energy into writing and counting and forgetting. Soon she started to relax, the tension easing from her body as she fell into a steady work rhythm. Not that she managed to forget his presence. She was keenly aware of him, especially when he started whistling. But oddly enough, the noise didn't spook her or make her heart thunder. It eased her mind, as if she liked having him close by almost as much as she'd liked kissing him last night.

She ignored the crazy thought. The last thing she wanted in her life, the last thing she needed, was to relax her guard where Houston Jericho was concerned.

She had to remember who she was and where she was and the all-important fact that a girl like Sarah—a nice girl like Sarah—had no business getting up close and personal with a man like Houston Jericho.

Even if she did like having him close enough to hear him whistle.

HE WASN'T WHISTLING.

The truth hit her the moment she returned from the back storeroom to hear the deep rumble of his voice coming from the front of the nursery.

"We'd be glad to do that...."

"That would help me out so much." The voice came from Edward Jenkins, a retired judge who lived out near the county line. He was a stern old man with beady black see-everything eyes that always made Sarah feel as if she'd done something wrong.

A feeling she'd had many times while growing up in Cadillac. Because she'd often been guilty.

But things were different now. She was all grown up and she didn't cause the same scandal.

She knew that, but damned if she didn't feel as if she were seventeen again and she'd just been caught red-handed toilet-papering the statue in front of the courthouse.

Tamping down on the emotion, she walked over, forcing a smile. "How are you today, Mr. Jenkins?"

"Fine and dandy thanks to the excellent service I just received."

"Service?" Her gaze went from Mr. Jenkins to Houston. "But we're closed today."

"But I just bought a dozen of those azalea bushes over there."

Her gaze went to Houston and he shrugged. "We're here so you might as well do a little business."

"You can deliver them first thing tomorrow. I'll be waiting."

"Deliver?" Her gaze switched to Houston again. "We don't make deliveries."

"What she means," he told Mr. Jenkins, "is that we haven't made deliveries in the past. This will be our first."

"Wonderful." Mr. Jenkins waved. "See you tomorrow."

"What are you doing?" Sarah turned on Houston the moment the bell tinkled behind the old man.

"Giving the customer what he wants. He wanted a delivery, so I offered a delivery."

"But I don't make deliveries."

"You should. People want full service and they're more than happy to pay extra for it." He held up Mr.

Jenkin's check. "Twenty dollars for maybe ten cents of gas and a little trouble. Not bad for a day's work."

"But I don't have a truck."

"I do."

She shook her head. "You can't just come in here and start pushing me."

"Who's pushing? I saw an opportunity and I took it. Isn't that what building a business is all about?"

"But this isn't your business. It's mine."

"Then you should be thanking me. If you advertise a little, you could make a killing."

"I don't want to make a killing. I just want to do my duty for as long as necessary, and then I'm out of here."

"So make a killing in the meantime. Haven't you ever heard of living for the moment?"

Of course she'd heard of it. She'd practically invented it in her previous life.

One that didn't seem nearly as far off and distant with Houston Jericho so close and staring at her so intently.

"Leave things alone. Leave me alone." Her voice softened and the desperation rolling inside her crept into the next word. "Please."

He shrugged. "Is that what you really want?"

No. "Yes. I've been doing fine, just fine, and I want to keep doing just fine. I don't need you making my life more complicated. I want to keep things simple.''

''You mean boring.''

''I mean simple. I go to work each day, I look after my grandma, and I go home. Simple.''

''Sounds boring.''

''It is. That's the point. It's boring and it's easy and I've fallen into a nice routine. I don't need you stirring things up.''

''Maybe you do.''

''What's that supposed to mean?''

''That maybe me leaving you alone isn't the answer. Maybe the answer is for me *not* to leave you alone.'' His voice dropped to a low murmur. ''You thought about me last night, didn't you?''

''In your dreams.'' She turned and busied herself spraying the leaves on a ficus.

''No.'' His deep voice came from behind a heartbeat before he forced her around. ''In *your* dreams. Your fantasies. You saw me last night, didn't you?''

No. The word was there on the tip of her tongue and all she had to do was open her lips and let it out. But she couldn't. Not with him staring at her, into her. She nodded.

''I saw you, too. I saw you all slick.'' He touched her cheek, traced the shape with his callused fingertip before making his way down the damp skin of her neck. ''As slick as you are right now.''

"I saw you," she admitted. "You were slick, too. And soapy." And aroused. He'd been fully aroused and she'd been ready for him.

"The shower scene. I've thought about it so many times. And the others, too. I can't help but wonder what you would look like in number five. What you would sound like in number six. What you would taste like in number seven."

"The same as the first three. All the same."

"Probably. But I don't know for sure. That's the damned trouble of it all." His gaze fired an intense gold as hot as the Texas sun and just as scorching. "I need to know, and so do you."

"I don't—" she started, but then he pressed a fingertip to her lips.

"Think about it."

He didn't touch her again or kiss her. He merely turned and walked away.

She expected to feel a rush of relief when the door shut behind him. Instead, she found herself walking to the door to stare out as he gunned the engine. The truck growled and spewed gravel as he pulled out of the parking lot. She caught his gaze as he glanced back, as if he knew she would be watching him.

The same way he knew she would be thinking about him. Dreaming. Fantasizing.

"I need to know, and so do you."

He was right. The need was there, fierce and gripping, and it was all she could do to turn away and finish the rest of her inventory.

But she did. She had to because, as much as she needed to know, she didn't *want* to know.

He lived and breathed in her fantasies and that was okay, because they were her fantasies. He wasn't real then. He didn't show up at her work unannounced, or touch her in aisle three or set up a delivery she couldn't possibly make without his help. The fantasies didn't upset her life the way the real man did.

She controlled the fantasies. She could think about him when and where she wanted, and those thoughts didn't affect her real life.

Even so, she couldn't seem to shake the memory of their kiss or forget the fierce look in his eyes just before he'd left the nursery. He consumed her thoughts for the rest of the afternoon, so much so that she actually forgot the time.

For the first time in twelve years, forever reliable and punctual Sarah Buchanan was late for her Sunday dinner with Grandma Willie.

"EVEN IF IT AIN'T THE champion himself." Hank Brister's voice echoed through the old barn as the man rolled out of the small office located at the far end. His wheelchair crunched hay as he made his way over to Houston. "You're looking good, boy.

Mighty good. As damned good looking as your daddy ever was.''

Houston ignored the rush of pride that went through him.

Pride? Because he looked like his father?

He felt many things where Bick Jericho was concerned, but pride wasn't one of them. *Hatred* because the man had never done right by him or his brothers. Bitterness because he'd not only been neglectful, but cruel as well. Confusion because he couldn't understand why. And anger with himself because he didn't want to know why. He didn't care. Because no reason was good enough for a man to deprive his kids of the love they'd needed so badly.

Back then. But Houston had stopped longing for his father's love a long time ago, well before the man had drunken himself into an early grave.

''You're looking good yourself,'' he told Hank Brister, eager to change the subject. ''Much better than the last time I saw you.'' He'd visited Hank Brister in the hospital when the man had first lost his leg to a vicious bitch of a bull named Harpo. One stomp on the man's thigh had ended his career several years back.

''I'm feeling better, that's for damned sure. Getting around pretty good, too, all things considered. So what brings you out here?''

''A wedding yesterday and Miss Marshalyn's

party in two weeks. I thought I might as well hang around here rather than make another trip back.'' He gave Hank the same story he'd given Sarah.

Truthfully, he'd intended to leave last night after she'd walked away from him at the wedding. He'd gone back to the bed-and-breakfast and packed up his stuff. Then he'd pulled his T-shirt over his head and smelled her on the material. And his brain had short-circuited.

He'd sunk to the edge of the bed, the material pressed to his nose, and all thoughts about the upcoming PBR finals had faded in a rush of heat. She'd been right there with him. The taste of her still potent on his lips. His fingertips still tingling from the feel of her soft skin.

He'd stretched out on the bed and given himself over to the image of her so soft and warm and ready. He'd fantasized then the way he always did when her memory managed to distract him, but it wasn't nearly as fulfilling as usual.

Because he'd gotten a taste of the real thing and he wanted more.

She'd not only kissed him, she'd gotten under his skin and fired his blood, and no matter how many times he played his favorite memory over and over in his head, it wasn't enough to slake the lust eating at his common sense.

He needed the real woman for that.

Which meant he had to get Sarah out of his thoughts and into his arms for the final four of the Sexiest Seven. Then he could stop thinking and fantasizing and wondering.

He would know. His curiosity as satisfied as his greedy body. Then he would leave Cadillac the way he always did, but this time he would be rid of the fantasy that had haunted him all these years. He could forget her for good and sever the one tie to his past. And then he could concentrate on his future. On breaking the championship record and proving his old man wrong once and for all.

In the meantime…

He turned his attention back to Hank.

"You still got that old mechanical bull out back?"

"I might."

"Think you can still run it as good as you did back in the old days?"

"Does a bear shit in the woods?" He grinned. "What did you have in mind?"

"I need to practice. To stay in top form for Vegas."

Hank grinned. "You came to the right place, boy. Ain't nobody gives a ride like me and old Nell out back."

Actually, Houston could think of someone who did, but he'd made up his mind not to think about her for the time being. She was the one who needed to think. To burn.

If she got hot enough, he had no doubt she would come to him. He just hoped it didn't take too long.

He'd never been a patient man when it came to something he wanted, and he wanted Sarah Buchanan.

Almost as much as he wanted that tenth championship.

"We can start first thing tomorrow if you want," Hank said. "I've got my boy Harley over there—" he pointed to a twenty-something man shoveling oats into a feeder "—to help out with the chores here and a foreman who oversees the ranch, so most of my time is my own."

"How about today?" Houston needed to slide his hand under the grip, feel the rope cut into his palm. Maybe then he could forget the softness of her skin. The warmth. "Right now."

"Harley!" Hank called out. The young man, dressed in worn jeans and boots, the sleeves of his plaid button-down shirt rolled up to his elbows, turned toward them. "Go on out back and pull the tarp off of Nellie. We've got an old friend here who wants to say hello."

"You sure?"

"I said so, didn't I?"

"Hot damn!" The young man grinned, shoved the

scoop into the large sack of oats and headed for the rear of the barn.

Hank grinned and turned to Houston. "Follow me."

"I'M SO SORRY, GRANDMA. I got caught up at the nursery and forgot the time." Hey, it was the truth. She didn't say she'd been caught up *with* the nursery, just *at* the nursery. She kissed the old woman on the cheek and headed into the kitchen to retrieve the dinner plates.

No more, she told herself. She was not going to think about him, or the way that his lips felt eating at her own, or the way his fingers had plucked at her nipple in the dark corner of the VFW Hall last night. Or the way he'd traced those lazy circles right against her—

"You look flushed, dear." Her grandmother's voice shattered the thought.

Sarah whirled. A plate slipped from her hand and crashed to the floor. "Oh, no." She dropped to her hands and knees and started to retrieve pieces. "I'm so sorry, Grandma. I know these are your favorite dishes. I can't believe I'm so clumsy." She gathered a few large shards. "Maybe I can glue it."

"It's all right." Grandma Willie hobbled into the kitchen and opened the trash can. "I'm more worried about you than a worthless plate." She eyed her granddaughter as Sarah deposited the pieces into the can. "Are you all right?"

Sarah put on her best smile for her grandmother, the way she'd been doing for the past twelve years. Oddly enough, despite the years of practice, the expression didn't come as easily tonight as it should have. "Why wouldn't I be all right?"

"I don't know. Maybe something happened that you're not telling me about." Grandma Willie eyed her as she rushed toward the trash can.

"What could have possibly happened? I've been at the nursery all day." Sarah dumped the pieces into the trash and turned toward the cabinet to get another plate. "Just counting inventory and watering plants and tallying the week's sales and counting inventory and—"

"You counted inventory twice?"

"What?"

"You said you counted inventory and then you said you counted inventory again."

"I did? Well, yes, I, um, guess I did. But the first time I came up short so I had to do it again, but then everything matched and so everything's fine. Really. Everything is A-okay."

Her grandma didn't look convinced. "You look jittery, dear."

Sarah's fingers tightened around the edge of the

stoneware and she willed them to stop trembling. "Do I?"

"You look like you have a fever."

Boy, did she ever. Unfortunately, it had nothing to do with an illness and everything to do with a certain hot and sexy cowboy and...

She sucked in a much needed breath. "I feel fine. Really." She wiped at a drop of sweat that slid down her temple. "I'm just a little flushed. My fan wasn't working at the nursery. I think the wiring's messed up." The lie came easily. Much too easily considering that she didn't lie to her grandmother anymore.

She never had to because she walked the straight and narrow. She paid her bills on time and opened the shop bright and early every morning and she went to bed at a respectable hour and she attended every chamber of commerce meeting and she helped out at the local women's shelter every third weekend of the month and she never, ever did anything irresponsible like forgetting her dinner date with her grandmother.

Until tonight.

Houston Jericho had not only unlocked her nursery that morning, he'd unlocked the door to her most erotic thoughts, as well, and they were now overwhelming her, interfering with her daily life and threatening her cover and—*stop!*

She closed her eyes and drew a deep, calming

breath. She could do this. She could keep on going as if everything was the same as yesterday and the day before that and the day before that. Just the way she'd been doing her entire adult life.

It was simply a matter of focus.

She fixed her gaze on Grandma Willie and noted the woman's concerned frown. And her trembling hands. And her tired slump. The past rushed at her as she remembered a similar look, and she rushed forward.

"Grandma, are you okay? Your chest isn't hurting, is it?"

"What? My chest? Of course not."

"You should sit down."

"I feel fine."

"Do you want some water?"

"I'm not thirsty."

"How about something to eat? I was late so you're probably starving. Your sugar's probably down."

"I took my sugar an hour ago. It's fine. I'm fine. It's you I'm concerned about."

"You should sit down, anyway. Please."

"But…" She started to protest, but then she seemed to think better of it. "Maybe I will sit down."

"Good. You just sit right here and let me get your dinner for you." Sarah helped her grandmother settle into a chair and headed off to the kitchen, her only thought on making the old woman as comfortable as possible.

At least that's what she told herself, and she actually managed to believe it for the next few hours as she and her grandma shared dinner and watched a few hours of television.

But when Sarah climbed into bed that night, Houston Jericho walked back into her thoughts, and the fantasy started all over again.

4

"THIS IS A ONE-TIME THING only," Sarah told Houston as she climbed into the passenger side of his pickup, the bed filled with Mr. Jenkins's large order of azalea bushes.

"This is good business."

"What do you know about the nursery business?"

"I know that for any business, it's all about making the customer happy. Mr. Jenkins looked mighty happy when I told him we could deliver his purchase. He even looked happy when I added the delivery charge to his bill."

"But I don't have a truck."

"You do today."

"Exactly, which is why today is a one-time thing. I can't be away from the nursery for deliveries."

"You could if you made them before you opened, or in the late afternoon."

"Would you stop with the suggestions?"

He shrugged. "Just trying to help."

"You're not. You're making me crazy." In more ways than one.

She was acutely aware of his close proximity. Of the firm masculine thigh only an arm's length away. If she wanted to, she could reach out and finger the hairy skin barely visible through the rip in the thigh.

If she wanted to? Okay, so she wanted to. But she wouldn't. Because Sarah Buchanan didn't do those things anymore. And she wouldn't do them until Grandma Willie was no longer living and breathing and Sarah had fulfilled her promise to the old woman.

Until then, she intended to be a well-behaved, modest young woman. The picture of wholesome goodness. Saint Sarah, herself.

Her gaze drifted to his thigh again and she licked her lips. And then promptly regretted it when she found him looking at her, his liquid-gold gaze dark and hungry and tempting.

"We'd better hurry. I have to get back."

"Isn't your cousin Arnie watching things?"

"That's why I have to get back. Last time I was out for a chamber of commerce luncheon, he gave away two gallon containers of Mexican heather and ten bags of potting soil in exchange for a new fan belt for his car. He's really into cars and he's not too good with money. But he's reliable," she added, suddenly feeling guilty for not pointing out his finer qualities.

If you can't say something nice, don't say it at all.

Her Grandma Willie's voice echoed through her head and she stiffened. She became acutely aware that she was riding through the heart of Cadillac in Houston Jericho's truck, in front of God and everybody.

There goes the reputation.

She shook away the thought. He was giving her a ride. End of story. It wasn't as if she was jumping his bones for all the world to see.

Not yet.

She ignored the sudden image of Houston beneath her, his body glowing with a fine sheen of sweat, his eyes piercing as she slid down his hard length in a ride that was far from innocent and blatantly carnal.

"Are you okay?"

"W-what?" Her head snapped around and her cheeks burned.

"You look flushed. Are you running a fever?" Concern furrowed his brow and a burst of warmth went through her. Followed by a rush of embarrassment because he knew what she was thinking. He looked into her gaze and she knew he knew and it made her face burn all the hotter.

"I'm fine." She adjusted the air-conditioning vent and aimed the blast of cool air at her face. Then she busied herself rifling through the stack of invoices she'd brought with her to keep her occupied while they made the twenty minute drive out to Mr. Jenkins's house.

Five minutes of staring at the same invoice and seeing nothing except that thigh out of the corner of her eye had her folding the blasted things and stuffing them into her purse.

"Whoever planted those hibiscus are just asking for trouble," she said as they passed the local cemetery. The familiar flower blossomed in the bright Texas sunlight. "Those are tropical. While it's hot here in the summer, the first cold front will whither them right up. Wildflowers grow best outdoors and they're less trouble to maintain."

"You really know a lot about flowers."

"You would, too, if you'd spent every day after school helping Grandma Willie at the shop. I was in charge of watering—that was back in the old days before I took over and added an automatic sprinkler system in the greenhouse. As I watered, I had to recite the plant's name and classification and a few characteristics." At his surprised glance, she added, "Grandma wanted to cultivate my green thumb the way she had my mother's. They used to play the name game when Mom was small, and so Grandma played it with me."

"But you didn't like it the way your mother did."

She shrugged. "I didn't like it *because* my mother liked it so much. I didn't want to be my mother. I couldn't be." Now, why had she said that?

Because as hot as he made her physically, there

was something oddly comforting about his presence and the fact that he was listening, and understood.

He'd longed for love as a child as much as she had. But while her grandmother had showered her with love, albeit the love she'd felt for her deceased daughter, his father had never shown him any sort of affection.

An image rushed at her of a young man, his gaze full of pain as he'd told her about his father and his childhood that night down by the creek. She had the sudden urge to reach out to him now the way she had that night. To slide her arm around him and pull him close until the pain faded.

She stiffened and fixed her gaze on a distant patch of flowers. "Bluebonnets," she blurted. "A perennial that thrives in full sunlight."

"What about that one?" He pointed to a small patch of white wildflowers.

"Ragweed. An unfortunate perennial that thrives in a warm climate. Allergists the state over owe their careers to Texas ragweed."

"You are good." A wealth of meaning filled his voice and she shifted to find a more comfortable position.

"I had to be, otherwise I would have spent Saturdays cooped up in the greenhouse. If I played the game and got everything right during the week, my Saturdays were my own."

"I bet you never missed."

She grinned. "Once in a while—when I was much younger—but I was a very quick study. Especially with my favorite day of the week hanging in the balance." Or rather, it had been her favorite day.

The one she'd planned for, dreamed of, relished because she'd been free of the greenhouse and her mother's shadow. "I would set my alarm for seven o'clock, pack my bag and head down to the river near Jackson's Ranch."

"I didn't know there was a river out at his place."

"It's small and private, and surrounded by so many trees that you can't see it unless you're right there. Anyhow, it was my favorite spot because there's all this carpet grass and a huge oak tree that dangles out over the water. I don't know how many times I climbed that tree and walked the branch out over the deep end. I used to pretend I was a tightrope walker in the circus or that I was crossing an unsteady bridge in the Amazon while fleeing a bunch of cannibals."

"Sounds exciting."

"It was, and it was an escape, albeit temporary, from Cadillac. I wanted out of here so bad."

"But you're still here."

She shrugged. "A girl's gotta do what a girl's gotta do. My grandmother wanted a carbon copy of my mother to follow in her footsteps. Someone who loved flowers and lived for the family business and that's what I'm giving her. I'm carrying on the family tradition.''

''But do you like it?''

''What I like doesn't matter. It's about my grandmother. I won't cause another heart attack.''

''Maybe you didn't cause the first one.''

''I was a constant source of worry and stress.''

''You were a teenager. That's what teenagers do. They worry their parents and stress them out.''

She cut him a sideways glance. ''I climbed a twenty foot flagpole and spray painted a mustache on the school's mascot.''

He shrugged and his mouth split into a grin. ''Okay, so you were a really wild teenager, but those exist the world over. They cause sleepless nights and a gray hair or two, but that's expected.'' His gaze locked with hers for a heart-pounding moment. ''Raising kids is tough, but it's not life-threatening. At least not for the average parent.''

''What's that supposed to mean?''

''That your grandmother wasn't the average parent. She was much older. It's understandable that her health wouldn't be as good as a woman thirty years her junior. Not to mention she had the added pressure of running her own business. I'd say her age and her workload contributed to her health problems more than anything you did.''

Sarah had told herself the same thing time and time again. But it hadn't been enough to ease her guilt or erase the image of her grandmother turning pale and blue and lifeless.

"I owe her. I could have been the one in the car that night. I would have been except that Grandma Willie grounded me and made me stay home to watch *Wheel of Fortune* with her. She saved my life, and now I'm saving hers. She has no reason to worry about anything, not the business and especially not me."

"When it's her time, it'll be her time. No matter what you do. That's the way of things. You're born and you die, and you don't have any control over the two. My father drank so much that he should have died a long time ago. But it didn't catch up to him until two days shy of my first PBR championship." He shook his head. "*Two* days. Can you believe that?"

"I'm really sorry about his death. I know you wanted him to see you ride."

"It wasn't that. He didn't have to see me. I just wanted him to *know*." He shook his head. "He said I would never do it and he died thinking he was right." His hands tightened on the wheel and she knew he was remembering the past and his father and she knew it hurt.

Don't do it. One touch will lead to two and two to three and...

She balled her fingers and kept her hands in her lap. Her gaze went to the passing landscape and a small area off in the distance where Bick Jericho had been laid to rest years before. It wasn't even visible from the road, but Sarah knew what it looked like because it wasn't far from her mother's resting place. When she took fresh flowers to her mother's grave, she always glanced at the patch of weeds and overgrown brush that completely concealed the small headstone that marked the grave.

"I've got some really nice potted palms." While she wouldn't reach out to comfort him with her touch, the sudden urge to do something—say something—to ease his pain overwhelmed her. "You should take one out to his grave."

He looked at her as if she'd grown two heads. "Why would I do something like that?" He shook his head. "He doesn't deserve anything from me. He never gave me or my brothers anything but a hard time."

"It's not about him. It's about you. You didn't go to his funeral." At his questioning glance, she added, "I didn't go, either. It happened so fast and everything was very low key that I didn't even hear about it until I saw for myself. I was visiting my mother's grave when they buried your father. It was a small funeral. Just your brothers and Hank Brister and Judge Merriweather, who recited a few words.''

''So?''

''So I just thought you might like to know how things went. Unless your brothers told you.''

''We didn't talk about it.'' He cut her a glance that said he didn't want to talk about it now. ''There wasn't anything to talk about. He died. We buried him. End of story.''

''It was a nice casket.''

''Dallas picked it out.''

''It looked like cedar.''

''Dallas likes cedar.''

''And the judge said some really nice things.''

''Good for the judge.''

''And your brother Austin said a few words.''

''Look—'' he pinned her with a stare ''—is there a point to this conversation? Because if there is, I wish you would just get to it.''

''There were no flowers, so after everyone left, I took him a small flowerpot of daisies.''

''Thanks, but you shouldn't have. He didn't deserve any flowers.'' The words were cold and cynical, but the brightness in his eyes told her he felt a lot more than he cared to admit.

''They weren't for him. They were for me. I felt good leaving them there. That's what funerals are for, you know. They're not for the person who passes away. They're for everybody left behind.''

"Since when?"

"Since always. They're a chance to say goodbye. You never said goodbye to him."

"I don't need to say goodbye."

"If you say so."

"So where's this place again?"

"Just over the railroad tracks.'' They lapsed into an uneasy silence the rest of the way there.

"You're here!" Mr. Jenkins met them out front when they pulled up. "This is so wonderful. I've already told Mrs. Hollister down the road and she said she's going in first thing tomorrow to get everything to redo her flower beds. She's been putting it off until her boys come home from college. One of them has a truck. But I told her you're offering delivery for practically nothing, and she was thrilled!"

"But I'm not—" she started, only to have him cut in.

"So was Ernestine Miller. She's the lady with the petunia garden over on Fifth Street. She's got rheumatoid arthritis and has a heck of a time driving. This new setup is perfect for her. You're a saint, that's what she said. What we all said."

"Um, thank you," she said, but the words held no enthusiasm. Deliveries? She couldn't make deliveries. This was a fluke. A one-time thing.

A test of her willpower, she realized as she climbed back into the truck and gave up the fresh Texas air for the scent of Houston. The sound of him. The sight of his handsome profile drawing her like a bee to a honeycomb.

"Mrs. McGhee got stung by a bee," she blurted when her hand actually slid a traitorous inch across the seat. The comment had nothing to do with anything, but she needed to talk, to divert her attention to something—anything—besides the fact that he was so close and she wanted him so much. "It made the front page of the paper," she rushed on, despite the strange look that Houston gave her. He knew. He knew she was searching for a diversion, but he wasn't going to help her by asking any questions. He was going to let her flounder around on her own.

Because he wasn't trying to deny the attraction between them. He didn't have to. To everyone he was the same old Houston. Hot, hunky, wild. She was different. She had an image to uphold.

"There was a picture and everything," she continued. "They had to call an ambulance. Speaking of which, the fire department added three new ambulances. The chamber of commerce had a car wash to help raise money for them. We made more than four hundred dollars. The high school band had a car wash, too, last week. I didn't have a car, but I went by and gave them five bucks, anyway...."

She rattled on for the next twenty minutes about anything and everything, determined to distract herself and keep from reaching out and kissing him.

She could. But she wouldn't let herself. And that was the damned trouble of it all. The push-pull. She kept pushing the need away, but it kept coming back. Stronger. More fierce.

By the time they reached the nursery, she was ready to scream. She scrambled out.

"It's not going to stop."

"I know it's not. Thanks to you. You heard Mr. Jenkins. He's already told all of his friends, and they've probably told their friends, and now everyone will be wanting me to deliver their purchases."

"That's not what I'm talking about."

But she already knew that. He was talking about the chemistry between them. The heat.

"I can't forget and you can't forget and it'll never change unless we do something about it."

"I can't." She shook her head, but there was none of the dead certainty that she should have felt.

"I want to sleep at night and I'm sure you do, too. And it's not happening right now. I keep thinking about you. About us. About the Sexiest Seven."

"What makes you so sure that I don't sleep like a baby?"

He gave her a pointed look. "Do you?"

Yes. No. Don't I wish. The answers rolled through

her head, but none of them quite made it to her tongue. She shrugged. "It doesn't matter. I really need to go." She started to shut the door, but he slid over and reached out, his hand holding the door open.

"You need me," he told her. "And I need you. Admit it and let's do something about it. Just admit it, Belle. Tell me what you want."

But she didn't want to think about what she wanted. She shouldn't think about it because she shouldn't do anything about it, because she shouldn't risk blowing her cover.

Then again, she'd almost blown everything already. With the kiss at the reception. With the kiss yesterday.

Because she couldn't forget the first three of the Sexiest Seven, and she couldn't stop wondering about the last four. About what it would feel like to step into the shower with him, or to kiss and touch in a public place, or to stroke him in a darkened movie theater, or to come apart in his arms in the close confines of an elevator with the world only a doorway away.

It was those fantasies that had driven her to kiss him those two times, and those fantasies that would drive her over the edge and possibly ruin everything if she didn't do something about them.

If she didn't turn each erotic dream into reality and regain her perspective.

The real thing wouldn't be as good, as consuming, as powerful. It couldn't be. It was the whole fantasy factor that was driving her over the edge.

And it wouldn't stop pushing and tempting until she stopped running and hiding.

Until she finally admitted what she really wanted.

"I WANT SEX," SARAH BLURTED into Houston's ear.

It was later that evening and he had just rolled over in bed to pick up the receiver after several rings.

"Sarah?"

"Yes. It's me and I want it."

"Hold on a second." He sat upright and threw his legs over the side of the mattress. He'd been stretched out on the small bed in the last available room of Cadillac's only bed-and-breakfast—there was a quilting convention going on at the local community center. He could have gone to one of the motels up the highway, or stayed at his brother Austin's place—Austin was single, though currently looking for a wife to satisfy Miss Marshalyn and win her land—but Houston had only intended on spending one night and he hadn't wanted to impose on Austin. Even more, when he'd decided to stay, he hadn't figured on spending so much time in his room. Tossing and turning. Fantasizing. Wanting.

He'd anticipated spending his nights, and any other free time, burning up the sheets and sating his lust with Sarah.

Unfortunately, she hadn't been of the same mind.

Until now.

"You want to have sex," he said, just to make sure he'd heard her correctly and this wasn't just an extension of the very erotic dream he'd been having.

"Not plain old sex. I want to finish the Sexiest Seven. The shower, the movie theater, the public rest room and the elevator." Silence followed before she added, "Are you there?"

"I'm here."

"I thought for a second you'd hung up on me."

"I'm hung up on you, all right, Belle, but the hanging in question has nothing to do with the phone and everything to do with me and the fact that I can't stop thinking about how much I want you."

"It's unfinished business," she said, and he knew she felt the same heat burning her up from the inside out. "Once we finish, things will get back to normal."

"Which means we should get started right away." His body throbbed at the prospect.

"We'll start tomorrow. I'll call you and we'll decide on a time and place." The phone clicked before he could reply.

Tomorrow.

She'd finally come to her senses. The knowledge sent a swell of relief through him. No more fantasizing about her. He was going to have the real thing again. He smiled at the thought as he stretched back out on the bed and closed his eyes. And remembered.

He could still see the beautiful picture she'd made naked and ready and bathed in moonlight. He could still hear the trickle of water and the buzz of insects and her soft moans as he'd slid deep inside her. He could still smell the intoxicating mix of fresh water and flowery perfume and wild female.

Tomorrow?

The heat burning between them had obviously burned up all of her common sense. There was no way Houston would make it through another hour without her, much less an entire night.

If she wanted to finish the Sexiest Seven with him, he would be more than accommodating. But they weren't waiting until tomorrow. He wanted her and she wanted him and they'd both admitted as much. As far as he was concerned, there was no better time than the present.

"Number four, here we come."

SARAH BARELY RESISTED the urge to snatch up the telephone, dial Houston's number again and beg him to come over right now.

She had neighbors, and the last thing, the very last

thing, she needed was for anyone to see Houston Jericho coming over late at night.

If she was going to do this—and she was—she intended to keep everything far removed from the life she'd created over the past twelve years. That meant picking a time and place where she wouldn't be recognized and there would be no threat to her carefully built image.

That meant starting with a shower in some motel or bed-and-breakfast in a far-off town where no one could possibly know her identity. Then she could start living out the final four, and gaining some perspective on the fantasies that had consumed her since Houston had rolled back into town.

She punched the Play button on her VCR and fast-forwarded to part four of *The Fantasy Factor: Sexiest Seven Places to Do It*.

The cheesy background music started, along with a brief narrative on the exciting aspects of showering with your mate.

The man peeled off his slacks and underwear, and Sarah wondered if anyone had ever died of sexual frustration.

She watched the man step into the shower and come up behind his partner. Heat coiled in Sarah's belly as he reached for the soap and rubbed the bar between his hands.

He lathered the woman's back, her shoulders, the

camera at such a close angle that the only thing visible was the glide of tanned fingertips over pale white flesh.

The video—which she'd ordered from a Naughty Nights catalog she'd come across during a floral convention in Austin—wasn't the least bit graphic when it came to body parts. The camera revealed nothing below the waist, which was why the classic video had been offered along with the newest line of sexy but tasteful scented lingerie. The manufacturer had set up a booth alongside myriad florists and nursery owners to introduce their new line. They had yellow baby doll nightgowns that smelled like daisies. Purple thongs that smelled like violets. A white lace honeymoon nightie that smelled like lilies. A racy red camisole that smelled like roses.

When Sarah had spotted the blast from her past, she hadn't been able to resist. She'd ordered a copy and she'd watched it a time or two. And she'd remembered. And fantasized.

Just the way she was doing right now.

Her skin prickled. Heat pulsed through her. She wished more than anything that she had a man's hands on her, slicking over her skin, soaping and teasing her nipples, slipping between her legs....

Tomorrow night?

She was insane and desperate and seriously doubtful she could survive the rest of the video much less a full twenty-four hours without sating the sexual frustration coiling inside her. She needed a man in the worst way.

But not just any man.

Of all the men she'd known in that short but busy bad-girl period of her life, Houston Jericho was the only one who lingered in her memory.

He was also the only one she'd ever made a pact with, and since Sarah had always been one to finish what she started, it only stood to reason that she would still think about him. Fantasize about him. Want him.

Not for long. Tomorrow night she would start to find her closure and then she could bury the bad girl she'd been once and for all.

Until then...

A woman's soft moan slid into Sarah's ears and prickled the hair on the nape of her neck. She watched as the couple kissed, open mouths pressed together, tongues darting in and out...

She needed a shower, all right. A cold shower.

She punched the Stop button on the remote and pushed to her feet. A few seconds later, she reached the bathroom. The quick turn of a knob and a blast of cool relief erupted from the showerhead. After peeling off her clothes, she stepped into the claw foot tub and pulled the curtain back into place.

Water pelted her, running in rivulets over her

heated flesh. She turned her face toward the spray and tried to clear her head. She needed to calm down and relax, otherwise she would never get any sleep.

And she had to sleep. She had a full day tomorrow at the nursery, not to mention even more deliveries scheduled, thanks to Houston and his interference.

His name stuck in her head and brought to mind all sorts of lustful thoughts. Of herself naked and panting and on her back, Houston between her legs, plunging into her and driving them both toward wild and crazy orgasms.

She shook away the notion, reached for the bar of soap and concentrated on lathering her hands. The feel of wet, slick soap made her palms tingle as she swirled the bar in her hands and bubbles squeezed between her fingers. She slid the soap back into the tray and ran her soapy hands up and down her throat, over her shoulders. But she didn't feel her own fingertips, she felt his. Trailing over her skin, circling her nipples, grasping the ripe nubs and twisting until she felt the pull of desire between her legs.

Her hands stilled and she drew a deep, steadying breath.

She wasn't doing this. She'd promised herself a long time ago that she wouldn't give in to her impulses, and she wasn't going to start now.

She reached for the shampoo bottle. It was tall and cool between her fingertips. *Cool,* as in the opposite of hot. If she could just focus on the sensation, she could forget the heat burning her up from the inside out.

She popped the push-up lid and was about to squirt the creamy liquid into her palm when the hard, smooth plastic brushed the ripe tip of her nipple. Electricity spiraled through her body and her nerves hummed.

She wasn't going to do it.

That's what she told herself, but her hands seemed to have a mind of their own. Her fingertips slid around the bottle, circling and grasping as she rasped the edge back and forth against her nipple. The cool hardness was a stark contrast to her soft, heated skin, and sensation spiraled through her. She played with the ripe greedy nub a few more heart-pounding seconds before touching the edge to her other nipple. It sprang to life at the contact, as greedy as its twin for a little attention.

She couldn't help herself. It felt so good and it had been so long. The edge of the bottle slid down, following the underside of her breast, the sensitive skin of her belly. The hard coolness trailed over her belly button and lower until she reached the vee between her legs.

Hunger spurted through her when she felt the edge of the bottle ruffle the soft curls that covered her mound. The sensation moved lower still. The hard, cool edge teased the slick folds and rasped over her clitoris. Her lips parted on a gasp and her knees trembled. She reached for the shower curtain to steady herself, but no sooner had she grasped the fabric than it was tugged from her hands. The rings rattled over the shower bar as the curtain slid to the side.

He looked as if he'd stepped straight out of her most erotic thoughts. He was naked from the waist up, his broad, powerful chest covered with a sprinkling of whiskey-colored hair. Muscles rippled as he reached for the button of his worn jeans. The fastening slid free, the zipper hissed and the material sagged on his hips for a split second before he grasped the edge of his white briefs and slid both the underwear and jeans down and stepped free.

His penis was hard and thick, the base surrounded by a swirl of gold hair that provided a stark contrast against his tanned skin. The same hair sprinkled his hard, muscular legs.

"Christ, you look beautiful. *Très belle.*"

"That's French. Since when do you speak French?"

"Since I took three years of it in high school. I didn't sleep through all those classes, you know. But don't tell anyone. It'll blow my image."

"I thought you called me Belle as in Jezebel."

"You thought wrong."

"I…" Her voice faltered beneath the smoldering

look he gave her and she swallowed. "What are you doing here?"

"Tomorrow is a long time away." His deep voice drew her attention and her gaze met his. Heat smoldered in the dark gold depths of his eyes and an ache went through her. "I've waited too long for this already. Thank God you didn't lock your door."

"I never lock my door. One of the perks of living in a small town."

"That makes two things I like about this town."

"What's the other thing?"

"You." He stepped in and took the shampoo bottle from her hands. But he didn't put it aside. Instead, he touched the edge to her nipple. It felt different somehow than it had a few moments ago when she'd done the very same thing. Especially with his gaze locked with hers and his body so close all she had to do was reach out and touch him.

"You like this, don't you?" She nodded and he grinned, rasping the edge back and forth until she caught her lip between her teeth to keep from moaning. "I knew you weren't half as good as you pretended to be."

"It's an act," she managed to say.

"Thankfully," he murmured, and then he caught her mouth with his for a hot, deep kiss.

The sensation between her legs grew until she

whimpered. She was so close to the edge. Another glide of the bottle and she would tumble over.

"Not yet." Strong fingers replaced the hard plastic. He touched her, slicking his thumb over her clitoris and rubbing while his finger slid deep, deep inside. "I want to feel you when you go wild, sugar." His gaze caught and held hers. "And I want to see you."

He moved his fingers, plunging and stroking. The pleasure was intense, but it was nothing compared to the brightness of his gaze as he stared at her.

Panic bolted through her and she caught his hand. "You're not following the video," she breathed, her chest heaving, her heart hammering. "It's sex in the shower."

"We're about to have sex. But first, I want you to come."

"We're both supposed to come."

"Ladies first." Despite her hold on his wrist, he moved his fingers again.

Sensation bolted through her and a delicious orgasm gripped her body. She caught her lip, fighting back the cry that worked its way up her throat, the same way she fought back the strange fear coiling inside her. A feeling intensified by the way he stared so deeply into her eyes.

She closed her eyes, shutting him out and effectively refocusing her thoughts on the hard muscle and warm skin pressed against her. She kissed him, tasted him, stroked him until he cried out this time. But not because of an orgasm.

He was close. So close. But she knew he wanted to be inside of her. And she wanted him there.

As if he sensed her urgency, he lifted her, hoisting her legs up on either side of him, his penis poised for entry.

But he didn't slide her down. He stepped out of the shower and set her down on the bathroom rug. Reaching over, he rummaged in his pants pocket and retrieved a condom.

She watched as he slid the latex over his bulging erection. He turned her around then and urged her hands onto the countertop, and then he entered her from behind, true to the end of the scene in the video.

He thrust into her, plunging in and out and driving her toward a second orgasm. At that moment, she caught his reflection in the mirror, his gaze dark and intense and searching. She closed her eyes, catching her bottom lip as an exquisite climax ripped through her, wave upon wave of sensation pounding her. And then she was floating.

From far away, she heard his cry as he followed her over the edge and slumped against her. His heart hammered in his chest, the rhythm keeping time with the frantic beat of her own heart.

She relished the feeling for several long seconds

before she gathered her control and pulled away from him.

"Thanks," she murmured as she reached for her bathrobe. "And I'll see you tomorrow."

"What?" He ran a hand through his hair and eyed her.

"Number four is over. We're done for tonight."

"Done?"

"You can let yourself out the way you came in." And then she bolted from the room before she did something really stupid like throw herself into his arms and beg him to take her all over again.

She wouldn't do such a thing because that was not part of the video or their agreement, and while she'd lost control for those few moments in the shower when he'd touched her with his hand and it had felt so good, she wasn't losing control again.

She was staying on track and maintaining her perspective, and she wasn't going to veer off the list again.

No matter how good it felt.

5

IT WAS STRICTLY SEX between them.

That's what Sarah told herself the next morning as she stood out behind the nursery and checked off the new arrivals. The early morning sun peeked through the trees and the birds chirped. Her second cousin, Arnie, stood nearby, talking a mile a minute as he hefted plants this way and moved pots that way to make room for the new stock. It looked and sounded like any other workday in small-town Cadillac.

But it felt different.

She felt different. She *felt*, period. The steady pulse of her heart against her rib cage. The press of her nipples against the lace cup of her bra. The slow glide of sweat at her temple. The steady pull of exhaustion on each of her muscles because she'd spent more than half the night reliving what had happened in the shower.

She completely ignored the fact that she'd spent the other half of the night remembering their first night together down by the creek. After he'd rescued her from Jake the Junior College Jerk. Before they'd made their pact and agreed to try out the Sexiest Seven with each other.

It had been a long time ago, yet she could still feel the warm summer air blowing over her skin. And taste the sweet mixture of strawberry wine and 7UP. And smell the crisp cleanness of the water. And see the handsome young man sitting next to her, a foam cup in his hand.

His thigh had pressed against hers as they'd talked. They'd been completely aware of each other. At the same time, she'd felt more comfortable than she had in a long time. More at ease. And so they'd talked about her life and how she desperately wanted to crawl out from behind her late mother's shadow. And how he wanted so desperately to outrun his father's criticism and prove the man wrong.

She'd never opened up to anyone the way she'd opened up to him that night. In more ways than one. She'd opened her body to him, as well. But it wasn't the sex itself that stood out in her memory. It was the little things. The tingle of awareness when his rough fingertips had caught a drop of wine cooler that had slid from the corner of her mouth. The way her stomach had done a triple somersault when he'd smiled at her as if she were the only girl he'd ever wanted in all his eighteen years. The way her heart had revved faster than his old souped-up Corvette when he'd tucked a strand of hair behind her ear...

Her skin prickled and she stiffened. She pushed away the memory and concentrated on counting the truckload of potted perennials and listening to Arnie, who helped her out three days of the week when she really needed him a full five. But she barely made enough to support herself and pay her overhead. A full-time employee was out of the question.

Even if business had picked up since word had spread that the Green Machine now offered deliveries.

She'd tried to set the record straight—that Mr. Jenkins's delivery had been a mistake—but then Susie Reynolds had offered to pay double for the delivery of a few potted palms, and Sarah had found herself stuffing the darned things into the back seat of her Ford Taurus. She'd managed to make them fit, but she knew there was no way she could squeeze into the small interior of her car the half dozen other orders that had come in yesterday. She needed a truck for that.

She needed Houston.

Not that she was about to call and ask for his help. Even if it was his fault she was in this predicament in the first place. She didn't want a friend or a helpmate. She wanted to keep carrying on the family tradition, running the family business and keeping up her carefully constructed front.

Which was why she'd agreed to finish the Sexiest Seven.

The thought stirred a vivid memory of last night. Her nipples pebbled and Sarah did her best to ignore the ache between her legs. While her feelings were perfectly natural, they weren't appropriate in the bright light of day.

"'...so I told him, 'Dawg, you're friggin' crazy.'" Arnie's voice pushed into her thoughts and she turned her attention to the twenty-year-old who'd been talking for the past few minutes while he helped her.

"There's no way in hell or heaven, or the in-between," he continued, "that I'm paying eighty bucks for a new chassis plate, even if it is chrome. And an original. And a once-in-a-lifetime find. 'Dawg, I ain't made of money,' I tell him. I work too hard for my green to go throwing it around. I've got responsibilities."

"Responsibilities? You live with Great Aunt Jean, who cooks for you and still gives you an allowance."

"Yeah, but I'm responsible with that allowance."

"You're broke."

"Not exactly. I've got twelve bucks."

"You just got paid yesterday."

"Jenny needed a new filter pump."

"And that took everything but twelve bucks?"

"While I was buying the filter pump, I spotted these sweet-ass seat covers."

"And?"

"And they were sort of expensive, on account of they were so sweet ass and all."

"I would think that an authentic chassis plate would be a lot more important than seat covers."

"And you'd be dead right. But the thing is, I didn't know I was going to happen into the chassis plate. I mean, how's a guy like myself supposed to predict something so huge? So awesome. So once-in-a-lifetime."

"How much do you need?"

"Eighty."

"I thought you had twelve."

"Actually, now it's a few bucks and some change. I stopped at Pancake World this morning for a short stack."

"You spent ten bucks on three pancakes?"

He shrugged. "You can't have a short stack without sausage. And you can't have sausage without hash browns. And nobody but nobody eats hash browns without a couple of scrambled eggs to liven things up."

"You had the Big Boy Special."

"What can I say? I'm definitely a big boy."

"You're going to be a tired boy. I expect you to

put in an extra six hours this next week—two hours for every day that you're scheduled to work.''

''Does that mean you're giving me the eighty bucks?''

''It means I need to have my head examined.'' She walked over to the cash register, punched the button and the drawer slid open. She counted out the money and slammed the drawer shut.

''Thanks, cuz.'' Arnie shoved the cash into his pocket. ''You're pretty dope.''

''Judging by the way you're smiling, I'm going to take that as a compliment. Now, get those flowerpots inside.'' She pointed to the row of bright yellow flowers on the far side of the truck bed.

''Man-o-man, an authentic chassis,'' Arnie murmured, a smile on his face as he filled his arms with flowerpots and started inside.

Sarah smiled and did a visual count of a row of bright pink begonias, jotted the number on her clipboard and flipped the page.

''I don't know about 'dope,' but you're definitely pretty.'' The deep, familiar voice sounded just to her left and a bolt of awareness shot through her. Her grip on the pen faltered and it slipped from her fingers.

A completely physical reaction that was totally expected, she told herself as she drew a deep breath and tried to calm her pounding heart. Houston Jericho had rocked her world last night, so it was only natural that she would get excited with him so near.

She expected the surge of need that went through her as she turned to face him. What she didn't expect was the strange rush of warmth she felt when he loaded his arms with several potted flowers and started inside.

A feeling that quickly faded into a rush of panic.

"What are you doing?" She started after him, following him inside.

"Carting flowers."

"But I've got someone to do that."

"He's at the cash register helping a customer."

"Then I'll do it myself."

"You can't do it. You're checking things in."

"I'll do it after I check things in."

"No sense in wasting time. I'm here, so I might as well do it."

"But you can't."

"Sure I can." He set the flowerpots off to the side of the back storeroom and started outside. "They're not heavy."

"But they're my responsibility. They're my job."

"Not right now." He planted a kiss on her lips as he passed her and her heart did a double thump.

"You kissed me," she said accusingly, following him into the storeroom.

"Yeah?"

"You kissed me. Just now. Here."

"And?"

"This is not sex."

"What are you talking about?"

"This." She motioned to the flowers and the nursery. "*This.* Carting flowers isn't on the list. We're supposed to follow the list. It's supposed to be strictly sex." She shook her head and stomped off toward the front of the nursery.

He caught her a few steps shy of the counter.

"Wait," he said in a low tone. "I'm not trying to piss you off or blow this image you've built for yourself. I just thought I would stop by and see if you needed a hand. It's the least I can do seeing as how I'm the reason you're swamped. I'm sorry about the delivery situation."

"Yeah, well, you're wrong." She faced him and suddenly the anger and frustration she'd been feeling faded into a surge of warmth. She frowned. "It isn't the least you can do. The least you can do is give me a ride for this afternoon's delivery."

"Sure thing. I'll be back at closing time."

STRICTLY SEX.

Sarah's words followed him out to Hank Brister's a half hour later. He needed to climb onto old Nellie and focus on something other than the attractive redhead who'd dominated his thoughts all morning.

She was right. Their relationship was strictly sex. Hot and heavy, fast and furious sex, but sex nonetheless.

He knew that.

So why the hell had it bothered him to hear her say it?

The question stuck in his head as he climbed onto the mechanical bull, gripped the hold with one hand and signaled Hank with the other.

The engine cranked, the bell *dinged,* and the metal monster cut loose, tossing him this way and that in a furious dance that stole the air from his lungs.

He held tight, letting his thighs feel the animal and his instincts guide him through the next move. A twist to the left, back to the right, again to the left, faster to the right.

Strictly sex.

Damn straight it was strictly sex. He wanted nothing more from Sarah Buchanan. From any woman, for that matter. He didn't have time for a real relationship. He never had and he never would because Houston Jericho wanted only one thing out of life— the next ride and the next win and the satisfaction and fulfillment that came from both.

That's what he'd been busting his ass for all this time, what he was still busting his ass for regardless of the fact that he was getting older and slower.

It was all about practice. About being the best.

Something his old man had known nothing about. Sure, he'd won a few rodeos in his day. He'd been good. But not half as good as Houston. He'd been stupid, too. He'd let a woman turn his head long enough to completely screw up his plans.

Not this guy.

Houston wasn't losing his focus, no matter how good the woman, or how sweet she smelled or how soft her skin felt or how she'd actually trembled in his arms—

The thought shattered as his hand slipped from beneath the leather strap and his legs came out from under him. He slammed into the ground and the air rushed from his lungs and everything went quiet and still. Except his heart. It beat with all the fury of the monster that had just thrown him.

"You all right, mister?" Harley Brister's voice pushed past the thunder of his heart and drew him back to reality.

Houston opened his eyes to find the young man peering down at him. Relief filled Harley's gaze and he grinned. "That was some kind of ride. I ain't never seen anyone that good. You looked just like you look on TV, Mr. Jericho. Even better."

"Get back and let Houston breathe, boy," Hank said as he rolled up to them. "Don't mind my boy. He's just a little starstruck."

"I seen you ride dozens of times on the TV,"

Harley said before he seemed to think better of it.
He chanced a sideways glance at his dad. "Not that
I'm into bull riding or anything. I'm going to veter-
inary college this fall."

"That's right," Hank said. "My boy's going to
have more out of life than a mouthful of dust and a
world of hurt like bull riding can give you. He's going to make something of himself." He extended a
hand to Houston. "You looked damned good that
time."

"How long did I go for?"

"You had great form, boy." He helped Houston
to his feet. "Just great."

"How long?"

"Six seconds."

"Shit." Houston damned himself for being distracted. But most of all, he damned himself because
Sarah Buchanan had said to him what he'd been saying to women for years now—that she wanted sex
and only sex from him—and that fact bothered him
a hell of a lot more than the fact that for the first
time in the twelve years he'd been riding on the pro
circuit, he'd lost his focus and busted his ass before
the eight-second buzzer.

TRUE TO HIS WORD, Houston returned just as she slid
the Closed placard into place on her front door.

She opened the doorway and watched him as he

strode toward her. He wore a dusty black T-shirt and worn jeans and boots that had seen better days, but he still looked hot. And sexy. And smelly.

She wrinkled her nose as he reached her. "Where in the world have you been?"

"Out at Hank Brister's. I'm training on his mechanical bull."

"It smells like real bull to me."

"Actually, it's not bull you're smelling. It's bull shit, and I sort of got thrown near a pretty big pile this morning." As soon as he said the words, she noted the stiff way he moved and she couldn't help herself. She reached out and tugged at the hem of his T-shirt. A huge bruise covered the lower half of his rib cage. "That looks painful. What happened?"

He looked as if he wanted to tell her something, but then he shook his head and shoved down the hem. "It happens. Everybody gets thrown once in a while."

"But not everybody smells like they just did a slow waltz with Toro."

He grinned. "I didn't have time to shower. I didn't want to hold you up."

"It's okay. I've been sweating all day. I'm sure I'm no spring bouquet, either."

"Actually—" he came up behind her, his lips close to her ear "—I like you all sweaty."

She knew he meant it sexually, but there was just

something about the way he said the word *like* that conjured all sorts of crazy thoughts. Like the two of them sitting side by side on a porch swing, or sharing a stack of French toast over at Pancake World, or walking through Cadillac Park on a Saturday afternoon.

Crazy, all right.

First off, she didn't want any of those things. Second, even if she did, she didn't want them with Houston Jericho. Why, her grandmother would have a coronary for sure if her granddaughter was to keep company with one of the notorious Jericho brothers. Their relationship was strictly sex, and it was strictly temporary.

As for *like*... She lusted after him. She craved him. She hungered for him. But *like* didn't figure in.

Not now. Not ever.

With that thought in mind, she climbed into the passenger seat and settled in for an afternoon of deliveries and self-control.

That was the key. She had to stay in control, keep her guard up and remember every reason why she shouldn't slide across the seat toward him. Making out in the front seat of a Chevy pickup was not on the list, and Sarah was as determined as ever to keep things in perspective.

Even when he stared at her as if he wanted to

swallow her whole. Or worse, take a nice, leisurely bite and savor her slowly, thoroughly.

"Are we on for tonight?" he asked her after they'd made the final delivery.

"What do you mean?"

"Number five."

"I have dinner plans with Grandma Willie."

"After dinner?"

"I have TV plans with Grandma Willie. I can't stand her up." *Even if she wanted to.*

She ignored the last thought. She was keeping things in perspective and that meant keeping her priorities. She'd promised to make up for being late the other night, and she intended to do just that.

"We'll have to do it another time," she told him as she climbed from the truck and left him staring after her. "I'll call you and we'll set something up."

She climbed into her car and tried to ignore that he was watching her. And that she liked it. And that she wanted, more than anything, to make plans with him right here and now for number five.

But her response to him in the shower had scared her a little and she needed time to regroup. They would get together again, but she would make sure that it was on her terms—her time and place.

He'd caught her off guard in the shower. That explained why she'd shied away from him and panicked when he'd looked at her. Sarah Buchanan didn't shy away from anyone, or panic. Not the real Sarah.

The good-girl Sarah was a different story altogether. She would have done just that.

But Sarah didn't have to pretend with Houston.

She wouldn't pretend and she wouldn't freak out again, because she would be the one calling the shots. In the meantime, she had responsibilities.

"I'M MAKING MY FAMOUS mashed potatoes tonight," she told Grandma Willie when she arrived at her grandmother's house a few minutes after leaving the nursery.

"You don't have to, dear. I'm not all that hungry. I had a late lunch with a few of the seniors from the ladies' auxiliary."

Sarah pinned her with a stare. "You're feeling all right, aren't you?"

"Of course, dear. Actually, I was wondering if you were feeling all right. You haven't been yourself."

"Of course I've been myself." Sarah laughed and prayed that it didn't sound as forced as it felt. "You don't need to worry. You just need to sit back and let me whip up a nice dinner. Then we'll watch television."

"I'm really not in the mood. I mean, I am—I don't have anything better to do—but surely you've got something else you would rather be doing."

"Actually, there is something." Sarah smiled. "I could give you a manicure."

"That's thoughtful of you, dear, but I really hate to impose—"

"We'll use the paraffin wax kit that I bought for your birthday last year."

The woman's eyes lit with excitement. "And you'll do the hand massage?"

"Of course."

Grandma Willie smiled. "I really haven't had a good hand massage in a while. And I do love the wax."

"It's relaxing and that's just what you need— something to relax you."

"Your mother used to give me hand massages after I'd put in a long day at the nursery. She always did this thing with her thumb right on the inside of my wrist."

"I'll see what I can do."

"Thank you, dear."

But Sarah didn't want her grandmother's thanks. She wanted peace of mind. And she found it that evening as she focused on her grandmother and forgot all about Houston and the wild woman lurking inside of her.

Until she walked into her dark, empty house later that night and found herself standing in the bathroom.

She remembered the previous night then. She re-lived it, touching herself the way he'd touched her, working herself into a frenzy just as he'd done the night before.

But the orgasm that followed was nothing com-pared to what she'd experienced the night before. It left her wanting more with a fierceness that both shocked and scared her, and made her all the more determined to keep her perspective and her precious control when they moved on to number five.

6

HE WAS THIS CLOSE to going up in flames. That, or dropping from exhaustion, thanks to the past sleepless night. Either way, he was hot and hard up and he needed Sarah and number five in the worst way.

She didn't seem half as anxious. She looked as calm, as relaxed, as well rested as ever when he stopped by the nursery the next morning.

He didn't get a chance to talk to her. The shop was full of people and she'd been busy trying to explain to Miss Esther all the reasons why she should stop planting her azaleas in full sunlight.

"Try planting them in a semishaded area."

"But I only have one flower bed and it's right in front of my house. I don't know where else to put them."

"Maybe I could stop by and take a look and make a few suggestions."

"That would be wonderful, dear. I do so love azaleas."

He'd caught her eye then as Esther had moved

away, but she hadn't done more than give him a se-
rene nod.

As if she didn't feel even half as hot, as frustrated
as he did.

The notion bothered him as he left the nursery and
headed out to Hank Brister's. He was halfway there
when he realized that the same blue Pinto had been
following him for the past ten minutes. He just
caught a glimpse of a female driver.

Suspicion hit him as he remembered the wedding
reception and Miss Marshalyn's efforts to point him
out to any and every woman in the place. He sped
up and hauled his truck around and did his damnedest to shake the persistent female, and then he headed
toward the house where he'd spent most of his childhood afternoons.

"It's not going to work," Houston told Miss Marshalyn when she hauled open her door after several
knocks. She wore the faded red apron he remembered so well. The smell of bacon and eggs drifted
out from the kitchen just inside, along with a certain
something that didn't quite fit. Something…funny.

"I don't know what you're talking about," she
said as she stepped back and he walked into the
kitchen.

He shut the door and barely resisted the urge to
throw the lock and pull the curtains, even though he
felt fairly certain he'd lost the blue Pinto and its per-

sistent driver. "The Heavenly Hook-Up Service that you and the other seniors have going down at the church." He shook his head, surprised at his own boldness where the old woman was concerned. But it didn't feel right being with Sarah and having other women chasing after him. He wasn't sure why, considering that their relationship *was* strictly sex, but it didn't, and so he was here to put a stop to the old woman's matchmaking once and for all. "It's not going to work."

"First off, it's called Creative Connections, and it has nothing to do with the seniors group down at the church. Why, that's the Lord's time. We only talk about it at the hairdresser." At his pointed look, she rearranged the platter of eggs and bacon she'd just placed on the table. "And sometimes at choir practice, but that's only when it's an extreme case and we have to help some poor soul in desperate need of a quick connection."

"Were there perms sizzling in the background when you were talking about me?"

She rearranged the bacon. "Actually it was a very passionate version of 'Amazing Grace.'"

"I knew it." He paced back to the door and peered past the curtains. The vegetable garden sat to one side. A huge flower garden glittered in the early morning sunlight. White sheets were draped over a clothesline, partially blocking his view. A perfect hiding place for someone if someone was, indeed, following him.

"Sit down, sweetie." She said the words she'd said to him every day when he'd brought her newspaper.

What he'd always hoped she would say, because she made the best eggs in town. Even better, she had the warmest and the best-smelling kitchen in town, and he'd liked just sitting there with her every morning. Not talking, just sitting and smelling and feeling the comfort of the gingham curtains and the rows of jellied preserves and her. He would eat and she would read, but every so often, she smiled at him over the *Daily Gazette* and made him feel as if he belonged.

This kitchen had been the one and only place that he'd ever felt such a feeling. He had the sudden image of some stranger sitting in this very kitchen once she sold out and moved to Florida. The thought bothered him a lot more than he wanted to admit. Not because of the land, but because of the house. This house. His house. At least that's what he'd pretended time and time again as a child when he'd longed for a home of his own.

"You look hungry," she said.

He tamped down the strange possessiveness bubbling inside him and focused on the old woman. He summoned his best frown—not easy considering he rarely frowned at Miss Marshalyn. Her constant interruptions and her headstrong ways left him feeling more dazed and confused than angry.

Not this time. He was fed up with her meddling and he intended to put a stop to it. "Don't try to change the subject. We were talking about your butting into my business."

"I thought we were talking about my eggs."

"Before the eggs. You put out the word and now I've got women following me around everywhere."

"Actually, it's just one woman. Imogene Asbury. You remember her, don't you? She's the same age as you. Light brown hair. Black eyes. Pleasantly plump. Her nose twitches when she smiles."

"You just described a hamster."

"Come to think of it, she sort of looks like one of those little fellas over at Pam's Pet Emporium. Sure, she's not your first choice, not with a pretty Persian sitting right next to her, but she sort of grows on you. She's so friendly and cute."

"And persistent," he said as he peered out the window for the familiar blue Pinto. "She would have followed me all the way here if I hadn't lost her by making a fast U-turn on Main Street."

"I thought you liked aggressive women."

"Aggressive as in straightforward. The type of woman to ask a man out to dinner. This woman's definitely got *stalker* written all over her."

"She's just lonely. Why, Myrtle told me that she hasn't been out with a decent man in ages. Just that pesky old Norman Ritter, but he's hardly a decent catch. He's got big ears."

"What do ears have to do with being a decent catch?"

"'Decent' implies good manners and good looks and a good work ethic. Norman's got good manners and a good work ethic, but he's only two out of three. You're three out of three."

He peered out the window again and looked for movement before passing a hand over his face. "I can't believe this."

"Dear, you look stressed. Sit down. Please."

He sank down into the chair, but he didn't relax. He couldn't because he had to tell the only maternal figure he'd had in his life to butt out. Even more important, he had to tell the most stubborn woman in his life to butt out, and he knew she wasn't going to take it very well. "Miss Marshalyn, I know you want me to stick around."

"Of course, dear." She patted his hand. "You belong here."

"That's the thing. I don't. I have an entire life away from here. I have to be in Vegas in two weeks for the PBR finals."

"You've already won that."

"You don't just do it once. You have to go back

every year to do it again. To prove you're still the best.''

"You already know that. What do you really need to go back for?"

"Because this will be my tenth win if my rides go well." If? He forced the question aside. "*When* my rides go well. That's a record. That's a big deal. Don't you see? I can't stay here." Can't? "I don't want to stay here."

"Not on an empty stomach." She pushed a plate at him. "Have some breakfast and then go take a nap on the sofa. Afterward, you can have some sweet rolls." She beamed and wiggled her eyebrows, obviously through talking about anything beyond her kitchen. "Homemade."

"You're not listening...." His words faded off as her words struck. Sweet rolls? He sniffed and the funny aroma made his nose wrinkle. "You made *sweet rolls?*"

"I'm making them right now." She walked to the stove and pulled open the oven door and the pungent aroma filled the kitchen, chasing away the appetizing aroma of eggs and bacon. "Mixed 'em up myself just a few minutes ago."

"Really?" He eyed the multicolored canisters sitting on the counter next to measuring spoons and a measuring cup. One held cinnamon and another flour and another salt.

A notion struck and he lifted the measuring cup and eyed the white granules. His nose wrinkled and he ran a finger around the rim. Bitterness exploded on his tongue when he lifted his fingertip to his mouth. "Um, Miss Marshalyn?"

"Yes, dear?"

"Exactly how many cups of salt go into a batch of sweet rolls?"

She laughed and closed the oven. "Why, you don't put cups of salt in sweet rolls. Only a teaspoon. You put three cups of sugar." She came up beside him. "Whoever heard of putting even a cup of salt in a batch of..." Her words faded as he handed her the measuring cup and she tasted what was left on the rim. "That's salt."

"That's what I thought."

"But it's supposed to be sugar. I always keep the sugar in my navy canister."

"I hate to tell you, but this canister's green."

"Green?" She squinted and held up the canister. "This is navy if I ever saw it." She opened the lid and dipped her fingers into the contents. Her lips puckered. "This is salt."

"I know."

"There's salt in my navy canister."

He started to tell her it was green, but then he saw the flash of fear in her gaze and he caught the words before they passed his lips.

She shook her head and her lips thinned. "Why, I bet it was that Constance Sinclair. She's always trying to prove to any and everyone that her pie is better than mine, and she knows I'm taking a pie to choir practice tomorrow night. Why, I bet she's even trying to impress Spur."

"Spur? Spur Tucker?" He remembered the wiry old man from the wedding reception. "Cheryl Louise's great uncle? The old guy who told anybody and everybody that he was here to find himself a filly to take back to his ranch?"

"That's him. Why, she knows I like Spur and she wants to show me up. She's always been competitive with me."

"You *like* Spur Tucker?"

"But she just thinks she's going to show me up." She went on as if he'd never said a word. "I'll teach her. I'm on to her. Why, I bet she switched my sugar and salt last week when I had the sewing group over here—we were finishing up the wedding quilt for Cheryl Louise." She shook her head. "She's good. Why, I was gone only five minutes when I stabbed my finger."

"You stabbed your finger?"

"A fluke accident. That needle looked so small and my finger was a good few inches shy. Anyhow, I was in the bathroom. That lying, cheating, sugar-switching—"

"You never used to stab yourself when you quilted."

"Accidents happen."

"Maybe you ought to talk to the doc about getting a stronger eyeglasses prescription."

Though none of his questions had gotten her attention, that one suggestion drew her full gaze.

"Why, I don't need a stronger prescription. I've worn the same one for years and it suits me just fine. My eyes are the same as they've always been and the last thing I'm doing is letting some doctor cut on them just because I've been making a few mistakes here lately."

"The doctor wants to do surgery?"

"They all want to do surgery. It's a scheme to milk my insurance."

"Doc McCoy doesn't strike me as the insurance-milking type. Maybe you should listen to him."

"And maybe you should have some eggs." She walked back to the table. "I bet Imogene can cook a mean egg. Not as good as mine, but close."

"Speaking of Imogene," he interrupted. "I want you to call her off."

"Nonsense. She's got her hopes up. She's so nice. And sweet. And she really can cook. Why, Myrtle told me she pickles her very own cucumbers with a teaspoon of honey, which makes them so divine. I've pickled my entire life, and not once have I ever even thought about using honey with my cucumbers. But they're wonderful. I tried them myself.''

''I don't like cucumbers.''

''Sure you do.''

''I don't like Imogene.''

''Sure you do. Everybody likes Imogene. She may be young like you, but she's got a good head on her shoulders. And she's as sweet as a plate of flapjacks and syrup. She'll make a perfect wife, and she can plow. She used to plow over at her grandpa's place. So if you and she decided to forgo the cattle and plant crops, you're all set.''

''I don't want your land.'' There. He'd said it.

She simply smiled and told him, ''Not yet, but you will. This is your home. This is where you grew up.''

Yes, he'd spent the best moments of his life here. But *inside,* not outside. He hadn't spent his time here running crazy on her land, or cutting the grass or rounding up stray steers. He'd left those chores to his older brother, who'd taken to the land like a stud to a mare.

Houston had been different. He hadn't looked at the animals as a practical way of making a living. He'd looked at them as a challenge. As a means to escape a dead-end town and his going-nowhere life. He'd looked at them as his chance to be different. Special. A winner.

And so he'd spent much of his time over at Hank's

spread, watching real cowboys—rodeo men who spent their time on the road and on the back of a bull or a bronc hell-bent on tossing them in the dust. Hank had not only ridden himself, but he'd trained the best, using the only mechanical bull in the state of Texas crafted specifically for rodeo training.

Houston's dad had trained on Hank's bull, and he'd been good. But not good enough. Not strong enough. Not determined enough.

He hadn't made it out of Cadillac the way he'd always wanted to, and he'd certainly never come close to winning even one PBR championship, much less breaking the standing record set way back when.

But his son was good enough, and he wasn't coming back to Cadillac. Not for good. *Never* for good.

That's what he told himself, but when Miss Marshalyn looked at him with that glimmer of hope in her eyes, he couldn't seem to make himself say as much.

"I don't think Imogene's the one for me."

"Do you have someone in mind?"

Did he? "No. I'd like to just wait and see what happens naturally." That meant following his heart, which meant he wasn't settling down in Cadillac. He was headed for Vegas and his record-breaking win.

"But if you would just talk to her, you might—"

"She's not the one," he said, cutting her off. "So tell her to forget any connection."

"I will not. You don't want a date. You tell her. It's that simple."

"You're the one who started this."

"For your own good, dear."

"Look—" he started, but she waved him silent as she always did.

"Okay. If you want me to tell her, I will. I just don't know if my poor old heart can take the disappointment on that child's face. Why, I'm liable to have an attack right there."

"Your heart is just fine."

"Now. But who knows if I put it under too much stress and upset that nice young woman?"

"But you'll do it."

"If you really want me to."

"I really want you to."

"If you're absolutely, positively certain that this is the best thing."

"I'm absolutely, positively certain."

"If you're—"

"Tell her."

"If you say so."

"Call her right now."

"Of course, dear."

SHE DIDN'T CALL HER.

Houston realized that a half hour later when he turned onto Main Street and passed the bed-and-breakfast. Imogene's blue Pinto sat out front. He gave up the notion of picking up a change of clothes and taking a quick shower, slumped down in his seat, bypassed the B and B and hung a sharp left. Sarah's nursery sat just up the street. He headed in that direction.

Imogene wouldn't think to look for him at Sarah's place. Not that that was the reason he was coming by. He actually felt bad about opening his mouth to Mr. Jenkins and talking Sarah into making the delivery. She was busier than ever—the morning rush he'd witnessed was testimony to that—and she could use an extra pair of hands. And a truck. And he could offer both.

He certainly wasn't coming by because he actually liked spending time with her, talking to her, laughing with her. Their relationship was strictly sex, just as she'd said, just as he'd agreed. And he was eager to prove to himself that she was just as anxious as he was to get to number five.

They were going to make some definite plans for the encounter starting right now. He wasn't scheduled to be out at Austin's place—he'd been helping his older brother in the afternoons—until later that day. Not that he could take too much time out at the ranch. Tending cattle simply wasn't his thing. He liked a more challenging pastime.

Soil and plants. Talk about a challenge.

He ignored the small voice. Keeping company with Sarah at the Green Machine was challenging because of the sexual tension that hummed between them. The anticipation. The heat.

It had been more than two days since they'd gotten busy in the shower, and he wanted her again. Hell, he'd never stopped, despite the shower. He could have kissed and touched and pleasured her all night long. He would have had she not looked at him with that closed expression and said goodbye.

It bothered him more than he liked to admit. But why? Was it hurt pride because she'd told him to leave and she'd been acting so distant since? After all, he was the one who walked away, who said goodbye, who kept his distance where women were concerned. He always had been.

Until last night.

She'd turned the tables on him and he didn't like it.

But there was more to it than that. The closed look she'd given him after the shower had been the direct opposite of the raw hunger she'd directed at him in the dance hall. The kiss that had followed at the wedding reception had been as wild, as reckless, as overwhelming as he remembered from twelve years ago. And he'd expected their sexual encounter to be as wild. He'd expected *her* to be as wild, as open. Instead, she'd seemed almost as if she was trying not to react, to feel too much. As if she was afraid.

And he couldn't help but wonder if she truly had changed. Because the Sarah he remembered would never have been afraid of her feelings. She would have wrapped herself around him and asked him to stay until the sun came up.

She'd wanted to. He'd seen it in her eyes, but she'd held back the emotion and sent him on his way.

So?

He never made sex an all-night deal. It was always temporary. Satisfying, yet straight and to the point. Because he couldn't afford "all night." Because that led to the next morning, and Houston Jericho didn't do the morning after.

He never had and he never would.

That meant there was more to the sex than just lust, and he'd vowed a long time ago to keep his head, and his distance, where women were concerned. His lifestyle didn't lend itself to a relationship. He was here and there and everywhere, always on the road, always focused. He didn't have time for more with any woman. And he didn't want more.

It was always about lust.

Now was no different. It's just that he was stuck here and he had more free time, and so it stood to reason that he would want to see her again. To fill up that free time with a pleasurable act. Not to mention, Sarah was safe. She didn't want more and he didn't want more and so they were a perfect match.

For now.

He focused on the last thought and turned into the gravel parking lot. It was all about right here, right now, and spending his lust.

He frowned as he pulled around back. There was a beat-up white pickup truck parked in his spot. A wave of jealousy shot through him as he pulled up next to the vehicle and climbed out. He'd rounded the side and was headed for the door when Sarah walked out, a large potted eucalyptus tree in her arms.

"Could you pull the tailgate down for me?" she asked, motioning to the truck.

He pulled the lever and shifted the door down. "Who's truck is this?"

"It's mine." She slid the potted palm into the truck bed, climbed in and pushed it to the far corner.

"You don't have a truck."

"I do as of eight o'clock this morning. I drew everything out of my savings account—what little I've managed to put aside—and I handed it over to old man Witherspoon."

His mind rifled back through his childhood and he saw the familiar truck bouncing and jerking down a back dirt road, the bed filled with a large metal cage that housed the old man's pride and joy—a pet skunk named Fifi.

"This is the skunk trunk."

"Fifi passed away last year and he's been trying to sell the truck ever since—it brings back too many memories and he wants to get on with his life. Anyhow, it's mine now and I've invested in a heavy-duty air freshener. It hardly smells like skunk at all."

He leaned in the window, took a whiff and winced.

"I just got it." She came up behind him and winced herself before putting on a confident smile. "A few days and I'm sure the smell will start to fade." She turned, walked back to the rear of the vehicle and lifted a potted plant. After climbing into the bed of the truck, she slid the large container to the rear and anchored it in place with a small piece of rope.

"I don't mind giving you a ride if you have another delivery," he told her.

She stood up in the bed and dusted off her hands. "Thanks to you I've got eight deliveries, and I promised Miss Esther I would go out and take a look at her place to offer some planting suggestions."

"I heard this morning. You could have talked to me."

"I was really busy. I'm still busy."

"That's why I'm here. I got you into this situation. The least I can do is help you out."

"True, but you're only here for two weeks, half of which is almost up. What am I supposed to do when you leave?"

The question hung between them like a challenge, and he knew then that buying the truck was her way of keeping her distance, and her control, where he was concerned. She didn't want to need him. To want him.

But she did, or so he hoped.

"You could have found something a little more reliable," he finally said. "And a little less smelly." He held out his arms to help her down and she stalled, as if the thought of touching him suddenly made her much more nervous than it should have.

She pulled back for several heart-pounding moments before she seemed to think better of it. She braced her hands against his shoulders and let him help her down.

He slid his arms around her waist and hefted her onto the ground. But he didn't let go of her. Instead, he stared down into her eyes for a long moment.

She had really beautiful eyes. They were a deep, rich brown that made him think of Miss Marshalyn's mouthwatering brownies. Hunger shot through him, but it had nothing to do with food and everything to do with the sudden need to be inside of her.

Right here. Right now.

The sound of tires crunching gravel drew their attention. The front parking lot was still visible from their position, and they turned to see a silver Cadillac Town Car pull in. Houston quickly recognized the two women in the front seat as Martha Jane Miller, the police chief's wife, and Jeanine Gilmore from the city council.

Sarah stiffened. "I really need to get back inside." She stepped away from him and started to move past, but he caught her hand and drew her around.

"So do I." He knew from the look on her face that she understood his meaning. "And I can't help but wonder what it would be like to slide a piece of popcorn down between those beautiful breasts of yours—" he flicked her top button for emphasis and let his fingers linger in the vee of her cleavage "—and play a little hide-and-seek with my mouth."

Her gaze darkened at the prospect, and for the next few moments, her panic seemed to fade. "So your movie food of choice is popcorn, huh?"

"Actually, my movie food of choice is you, darlin'."

"I—"

"Mornin' Sarah!" Martha Jane Miller's voice rang out, followed by the slam of doors as both women climbed from the car.

Panic lit Sarah's gaze and she tugged away from him. "You have to go. I've got work to do."

"When?"

"When what?"

"When do we get together again?"

"I'll call you."

"You're stalling." He caught her gaze. "Don't be afraid, Sarah."

"I'm not afraid. Friday night," she blurted. "The Majestic."

"The Majestic?"

"One of the theaters over in Cherry Blossom Junction. They're having a John Travolta film festival."

"That's a thirty-minute drive. Why don't we go to the Twin Diamonds right here in town?"

"And have everyone in town see us?" She shook her head and tried to pull her hand free, but he wasn't about to oblige her. Not yet. Not even with two of the city's biggest gossips fast approaching. "That's not a good idea."

She was right, but damned if the notion didn't bother him, anyway.

He grasped her hand firmly. "I'll pick you up."

She tried to tug free without making a scene. "I think it's better if we just meet there."

"There's no reason for you to drive all that way by yourself. That's crazy."

She stopped trying to resist and leveled a stare at him. "This isn't a date."

"Damn straight it isn't." Houston Jericho didn't *date*. Dating implied long term, at least in his book, and he didn't have the time to invest in a woman for the long haul. "This isn't about dating. It's about safety."

"Maybe so, but that's not what everyone in town will think when they see us together. They'll think 'date.'" She shook her head and lowered her voice. "The less we confuse the two, the better for everyone. I don't want to arrange anything other than when and where, and I don't want to hold hands."

She tugged loose and he let her go this time, despite the sudden urge to haul her into his arms, kiss her senseless and give the two old biddies a few feet away something to really wag their tongues about.

"The Majestic, then," he said. "Friday. Eight o'clock."

7

CHERRY BLOSSOM WAS a typical small Texas town located a good twenty minutes north on Farm Road 291. Small, but not minute like Cadillac. It had twice the population, as well as twice the number of grocery stores, feed stores and movie theaters—namely two of each.

The Majestic catered to an older set while the Big Bopper across town featured the latest teen movie. The billboard he'd passed on his way into town always had advertised the Big Bopper's feature as a beach movie starring a current teen heartthrob.

Thankfully.

That put the Majestic's parking lot only half full. He turned into a spot, killed the engine and climbed out of his truck. After rounding the corner of the building, he walked toward the marquis, where Sarah stood waiting for him.

She wore her usual subdued colors. Her navy skirt was soft and thin and fell in soft folds to mid calf. She wore a modest white blouse, her hair pulled back in a ponytail. She looked so sweet and wholesome

and conservative…so unlike the wild girl he remembered, her hair hanging loose, her cheeks flushed
from excitement, her jeans skin-tight, her blouses
low-cut, her bright red boots polished to a fine sheen,
and her eyes sparkling.

"I was starting to think that you weren't going to
make it." She glanced at her watch. "The movie's
about to start."

His gaze caught and held hers and he saw the fire
in the warm chocolate depths of her eyes. "I
wouldn't miss it for anything."

For a split second, he thought she was going to
shy away from him. She wore the same look of panic
she'd worn in the shower. As if the chemistry between them was too overwhelming and he stirred a
response that somehow frightened her.

The notion faded as she smiled. "Then we'd better
get inside."

"My plan exactly." The comment drew a soft
smile from her and she seemed to relax. "Now, let's
go. I don't want to miss any of this." He ushered
her toward the ticket counter.

"I didn't know you liked John Travolta that
much," she said.

"I don't." He slid the money across the counter,
ignoring the five she held out, and then took the tick-
ets and led her from the ticket counter. "This isn't

about John. It's about sex.'' He turned, his gaze locking with hers. ''Isn't it?''

''Um, yes.'' She nodded and let out a deep breath. ''I'm so glad to hear you say that. It's really important that we keep things in perspective. I mean, it's not that I don't like you.''

''I say you like me a lot.''

''Maybe. And maybe not. It doesn't matter. Don't you see that?''

He saw it, all right, and he didn't like it one bit. And that was the damned trouble of it all, because Houston couldn't afford to like Sarah. He didn't want to like her any more than she wanted to like him.

It had to be just sex.

A few minutes later, he steered her into the dark theater. Sure enough, the place was only half full. Just enough people to make things interesting, but not enough to get in the way of what he had in mind.

He ushered her up the staircase to the last row at the very top. The lights dimmed just as they sat down. The screen came alive and sound poured from the speakers as the previews started. He had half a mind to slide his arm around her and pull her close. That's what she expected. What he should have done. But the devil was in him right then and so he held back.

Waiting.

Letting the tension build.

The movie started, but he knew she wasn't watching. He felt her gaze slide to his profile every few minutes, as if to say *Hurry up, wouldya?*

He would. But not yet.

He settled back in his seat, willed his body to relax and fixed his gaze on the screen. They were a good halfway through the movie before he reached his limit and reached out.

He slid his arm around her shoulders and shifted in his seat. With his free hand, he reached over and touched her thigh. His fingers bunched, gathering the hem of her skirt until he'd pulled the material up over her knee. Fingertips touched warm, soft skin and desire bolted through him. She didn't so much as look at him, as if she were dead set on ignoring him the way he'd ignored her.

She stared at the screen, her bottom lip caught between her teeth as if it was all she could do to keep still.

He trailed his hand up the inside of her thigh, relishing the warmth of her skin. His erection grew, pushing against the crotch of his jeans until he thought he would surely bust the zipper.

Under the demure skirt, she wasn't wearing any panties. The realization sent a spurt of hungry desire through him and suddenly he couldn't get to her fast enough. She was still every bit the wild child she'd been back then. She just hid it better now. From everyone except him.

He touched the wet heat between her legs. Her juices drenched his finger as he slid into her. Her eyes closed and her head tilted back and he waited to hear the familiar cry that had always driven him wild during the three encounters they'd had.

She hadn't said a word during the shower enounter, but tonight would be different. He wanted to hear her, to know she felt as good as he thought she did.

He slid into her over and over, working the soft, tender folds. Her legs trembled and her fingers clenched the armrests, but she didn't make a sound.

Tonight she wouldn't hold back.

A rainbow of colors from the screen played over her expression, which left no question in his mind as to what she was feeling. Desire parted her lips. Excitement flared her nostrils.

"Move for me," he murmured into her ear, his tongue darting out to trace the shell of her ear. She trembled beneath his touch. *"Move."*

Several heartbeats ticked by before she seemed to gather her strength. She shifted in her seat, drawing him deeper. He slid his finger in and out, making her squirm and gasp, over and over until she exploded. Her body milked his finger and tremors shook her, but she still didn't so much as whimper. She held her bottom lip, her eyes closed, her face drawn in a tight, closed expression.

He withdrew and worked at the button of his jeans. The fastening popped open and he pushed the zipper down. His erection sprang forward. The seats in front of them hid everything below chest level and he knew that no one could see him. But they were there. So close. The notion stirred his blood almost as much as the beautiful woman sitting next to him.

He pulled a small foil packet from his pocket and slid on the condom, then urged her out of her seat and onto his lap.

She sank down onto him in one swift motion that stalled the air in his lungs and sent a burst of pleasure to his brain. He didn't breathe for several heartbeats. He merely sat there feeling her pulse around him.

Her skirt fell around them, hiding the fact that he was deep inside her.

A groan rumbled from deep in his throat, so loud he knew someone had to hear. But no one turned around.

Not that he cared. With her so wet and tight around him, he didn't care if the entire world looked on.

He slid his hands under her skirt and gripped her hips. He started to move her, but she took the lead. She moved her pelvis, riding him, her hands braced on the armrests on either side.

She rode him so hard and so good that he almost forgot his objective. Almost. But this wasn't about his own orgasm. It was all about hers. About driving her over the edge and giving her such exquisite sensation that she would want even more. And more. And she wouldn't—no, she couldn't—hold back.

He slid his hands around and touched the soft curls at the vee of her legs. He explored her, feeling his erection where it disappeared into her hot, tight body. Moisture coated his fingertip and he spread it along the already slick folds. He stroked her, rasping her hot spot until it swelled and throbbed and her body tightened around his. She moved faster and he moved faster until she arched her back.

He pressed that sweet spot then and she cried out, the sound barely muffled as he twisted her around and caught her mouth with his own. He kissed her hard and deep as tremors racked her body and she climaxed. Her insides pulsed in a delicious rhythm that sent him over the edge into his own mind-blowing orgasm.

His heart thundered in his chest, the sound filling his ears and blocking out everything around them for several long moments. Then his breathing calmed and his blood slowed and the voices of John Travolta and his leading lady finally pushed past the frantic beat of his heart.

He didn't want to move and he certainly didn't

want to move her. She felt too good surrounding him, her body warm and wet and…*home.*

He pushed aside the crazy thought just as she pushed away from him. She settled back into her seat and straightened her skirt as he fastened his jeans and tugged his zipper back up.

And then she stood up.

"Where are you going?"

"Home. I've got an early shipment coming from Austin. Perennials."

He caught her hand and tugged her around. "You've got to be friggin' kidding me."

"Our business here is finished."

"The movie's not done yet."

"It's not about the movie. You said so yourself."

"Then I'm not done yet." He eyed her. "Sit down and hold my hand."

"This isn't a date. This is number five." She licked her lips still swollen from his kiss, and he barely resisted the urge to tug her down and kiss her again. And again. And again.

She would fight him. He knew it from the closed expression on her face and the determination in her eyes, and so Houston did the only thing he could at that moment.

He let her go.

HOUSTON MEANT TO GO BACK to the bed-and-breakfast, despite that it was early in the evening and the town was still alive. But when he reached the corner just a few houses away, he spotted Imogene pulling into the motel parking lot and so he turned his truck around and headed out to Hank's.

He needed to focus in the worst way, to forget that he'd let Sarah walk away from him, to remember why.

Because it *was* just sex between them, and that's all he wanted.

Harley was pitching hay in the rear of the barn when Houston arrived.

"Hey, there, Mr. Jericho!" the young man called out.

"Your dad around?"

"He's up at the house. You here to ride?" His eyes lit with the same excitement Houston had seen that first day when Hank had told him they were firing up old Nell. A look that promptly faded when his dad rolled into the barn.

"'Course he is," Hank said as he rolled up to them. "I saw you come up the road," he said to Houston. "Let me get the generator cranked up in the tack room and you can climb on." Hank disappeared into a nearby doorway.

"You can watch," Houston told Harley when the young man turned back to his chores.

"That's okay. I've got work to do," he said, but

Houston got the distinct impression that there was more than just a bale of hay holding him back.

"I don't mind. It won't bother me."

"I'm not really into bull riding that much. My pa says he wants more for me than a bunch of bruised ribs and a mouthful of dust."

"And what do *you* want?"

Harley's head snapped up. "What do you mean?"

"You've told me what your dad wants for you, but what do you want?"

"You heard my dad. I'm going to veterinarian school."

"I heard him, but I didn't hear you."

"I don't know the first thing about riding a bull."

"Neither did I, but I learned."

"I could never be that good."

"You never know if you don't try."

The young man seemed to think for a minute, and Houston had the impression he was about to say something when Hank called out, "She's ready to rip!"

Houston tied on the worn leather chaps he'd pulled out of the back of his truck. He dusted the legs and pulled his glove from his pocket. Stuffing his hand inside, he walked toward old Nell and climbed on.

"Open her up!" Houston yelled, holding on to the cinch strap for all he was worth with one hand, his other poised to counter his balance. The mechanical bull jerked this way and reared that.

He held on, his grip determined as the machine twisted and turned and jerked. His thighs were tight, his knees locked in the form that had won him so many championships as he focused his body on the ride. On getting faster. Better.

The damned thing was, he couldn't focus his mind. He couldn't think about the bull and nothing but the bull. Instead, he thought about Sarah, he saw her closed expression before she'd walked away from him. He felt the unease build inside him because he'd had half a mind to go after her.

She was pulling back on purpose. Pushing him away. Keeping her guard up with him the way she did with everyone else.

So?

So it bothered him. It bothered him a hell of a lot more than it should have considering the only thing he wanted was to speed up his reaction time and sweep this year's PBR finals.

Yep, that's what he wanted, all right.

That and to complete the list with Sarah.

He sure as hell didn't want to hold her hand in public just for the sake of hand-holding, or go to the movies with her just because he liked feeling her next to him, or help her out at her nursery because he actually liked the quiet and the calm of the damned place.

He lived for excitement. For fast times and fast women and the roar of an enthusiastic crowd—

The thought stalled as his body veered too much to the right, the bull went to the left, and he found himself airborne.

He slammed into the ground, but he didn't stay down, despite his muscles that cried from the impact. Hauling himself to his feet, he turned toward the animal again.

And again.

And again.

An hour passed, then two, then three, until Houston was bruised and battered and felt as if he'd tangled with a real bull rather than a mechanical monster.

"Hold up," Hank called out as Houston started to climb back on again. "It's past midnight. I think we ought to call it a night. My arm's tired and you have to be this close to passing out."

"One more time," he gasped.

Hank eyed him for a long moment, as if he saw Houston's thoughts. As if he understood. "Sometimes the best thing you can do is back off for a little while."

The man was right. As far as the bull riding went.

Houston wasn't in any shape to keep getting his ass beat.

As for Sarah...forget backing off. That's what he'd been doing the past few days. Whenever she pulled back, so did he. She shut him out and he let her.

No more. It was time for him to step up, to get close. So close she couldn't pull away.

Maybe then he could stop wondering what she would look like completely open and uninhibited in his arms. He would know, his curiosity as satisfied as his lust. Maybe then he could regain his precious focus.

He had to, otherwise he was certain to make a poor showing in Vegas, and Houston never made a poor showing. He gave it his all, no matter how angry or fed up or just plain tired he was. He thrived on winning and he wasn't going to stop now.

That would mean following in his father's footsteps, and Houston wouldn't do that.

Not now. Not ever.

8

SHE WASN'T GOING TO SHUT him out tonight.

Houston made that promise to himself as he walked into the football stadium where the Cadillac Comanches were playing their arch rival, the Hondo Hogs, in a summer practice game. It seemed as if the entire town had turned out for the event. The stands overflowed. People crowded around the concession stands.

He spent a full ten minutes searching before he finally spotted her near the Sno-Kone stand. She sat behind a large table. A white banner was draped along the front, Cadillac Chamber of Commerce printed in navy-blue script. Platters of plastic-wrapped cookies, cakes and pies crowded the top.

If he hadn't seen it with his own eyes, he never would have believed it.

Sarah Buchanan, wild child and the most exciting woman he'd ever had the pleasure of sipping home-made wine coolers with, was hosting a bake sale on behalf of the fine, upstanding citizens who used to gossip about her.

An act. A carefully played act to fit in and fulfill a promise.

That's what he told himself. But the truth of the matter was, she didn't just play the part of the classic good girl, she looked it with her khaki slacks and white no-nonsense button-down blouse. Her hair was pulled back at the nape of her neck, her face devoid of makeup. And she wore a huge, pleased-to-meet-you smile.

She looked as fresh and wholesome as a glass of milk.

Nothing like the girl she'd been, yet he knew the real Sarah lay just below the surface. She'd told him as much that night at the dance hall. And over the past few days, he'd seen proof in the shower and the movie theater. But while she'd taken her pleasure, there'd been a measure of control to her actions. And her reactions. She'd gone only so far, and then she'd pulled back. And then she'd held back. Like last night when she'd come apart at his fingertips without letting out so much as a whimper.

Nothing that would alert anyone that Sarah was anything but the straitlaced lady she appeared to be. As he watched her hand out samples of cookies to a group of seniors who'd come over from the local retirement home, he couldn't help but wonder if she truly had straightened up her act the way everyone seemed to think.

Maybe.

As if she sensed his presence, her gaze lifted and locked with his. Her cheeks colored and her backbone stiffened and she actually looked nervous.

Nervous? Nah. She'd never seemed nervous, no matter what they did, how far they went, or how hard he pushed her. She'd reveled in every emotion, eager for more.

Or rather, she used to.

She would again. Tonight.

Houston had made up his mind to prove to himself that all the years he'd carried her memory with him hadn't been for nothing. He needed to know that she truly was different from all the other women in his life. While she had a wild streak, she also had heart. And in that heart, she felt something for him that went beyond lust.

He wasn't sure what that something was—compassion, kinship, affection…maybe all three. He didn't know, but he wanted to know, to feel *connected,* the way he'd felt when they'd sat on the hood of his Corvette, sipped homemade wine coolers and talked.

That night had been only the second time in his life he'd revealed his dreams of riding the pro-rodeo circuit.

The first had been when he'd been just a kid. He'd wanted to be a cowboy like the next four-year-old.

But for him it had been more than a child's fantasy. He'd felt the calling even then when he'd stared at the belt buckle his father had kept on the top of his scarred dresser. It had been shiny and big, and Houston had wanted his own more than he'd wanted anything, even the red wagon Miss Marshalyn had given him for Christmas that year.

He'd told his father as much, but the old man had merely taken a swig from his bottle of Jack Daniel's and said the words that would haunt Houston for the rest of his life.

"Take a good look, boy, 'cause this is as close as you're ever gonna get to one of these. You ain't goin' nowhere and you ain't goin' to do a dad-blamed thing with your life. This small shit-ass town is it. There ain't no sense wantin' more. You just ain't good enough. You'll never be good enough."

Worse than the words had been the sick feeling in his stomach. The doubt. The fear. That maybe, just maybe, his old man was right.

Houston forced the notion away. His old man was wrong. He always had been and he always would be, and Houston intended to prove it. He intended to accomplish the one thing his father had always talked about doing—breaking the standing record of ten consecutive PBR championships.

Funny, but the notion didn't make his heart beat nearly as fast as the sight of Sarah when she handed over a plate of chocolate cupcakes to one of the old women from the seniors' group.

Her smile widened. Two dimples cut into her cheeks and her nose crinkled and her eyes lit with warmth. The sight hit him like a good kick to the middle and his breath caught. He had the crazy thought that he would trade every one of his championships if she would smile at him like that just once.

Hell's bells, he'd definitely hit the ground one too many times. The *last* thing he wanted from Sarah was a smile.

He wanted to shake up her calm, conservative exterior and bring out the wild woman he remembered from their first three encounters so long ago. She'd moaned with satisfaction down by the riverbank that first night. She'd cried with it during their second time together. And she'd practically howled during the third. She'd been vocal and out of control and completely uninhibited.

While she'd come out of her newly constructed shell enough to proposition him and hold her own in the shower and the movie theater, she was still holding back. Still maintaining her control. Still putting up a front.

No more.

He wasn't going to let her hold back, nor was he

going to let her name the time and place for their sexual encounters.

Houston was taking matters into his own hands the way he always did, and going after what he wanted. And he wanted Sarah Buchanan. The *real* woman. Under him. Pulsing around him. Screaming her pleasure.

And there was only one way to do that. He intended to make her hot enough, hungry enough, so that she lost her precious control and unleashed the wild woman within.

Starting right now.

"I'LL TAKE ONE."

The deep voice slithered into Sarah's ears. Her hands froze near the cash box where she'd been organizing change. Her head snapped up, and her gaze locked with a pair of brilliant, whiskey-gold eyes.

Her mouth went dry and her lips parted and her stomach fluttered. The urge to taste him hit her hard and fast, regardless of the fact that they were surrounded by crowds of people and she was not the sort of girl who went around tasting men. Even handsome men like Houston Jericho.

Especially handsome, wild men like Houston Jericho, who made her cheeks flush and her nipples tingle and her thighs ache.

He was just so close. And so warm. And he smelled

so good. And her lips couldn't help but tingle at the prospect of sampling his.

"Cake, pie or cookie?" she blurted, eager to keep her traitorous mouth busy. "I have all three. And then, of course, you have to pick what kind you want. If it's a cake, I've got coconut cake, red-velvet cake, carrot cake, chocolate cake, apple spice cake—"

"A kiss. I'll take one." He handed over a five. "Maybe two if the first one is really good."

"This is a bake sale."

He arched an eyebrow at her. "I thought you forfeited the bake sale idea in favor of a kissing booth. Isn't that what you said to Wes at the wedding reception?"

"I said I would *consider* the idea of a kissing booth as a possible fund-raiser. The bake sale was already scheduled." She drew a shaky breath and tried to calm her frantic heartbeat. *Not here. Not now. No.*

He shook his head. "That's a shame. I really wanted that kiss."

She reached for a nearby platter and held it up. "You'll have to settle for a dozen chocolate chippers courtesy of Camille Skeeter—she's our secretary— from Skeeter's Pharmacy. That, or you can pick out a cake or a pie. I've already told you most of the cakes we have. As for pies…" Her gaze dropped to the two sitting nearby. "All I have left out here is apple, but I do have some peach and strawberry over in the storeroom.''

''I'm sort of partial to strawberry.''

''Then hold tight and I'll be right back.'' Sarah thanked the powers that be for a convenient escape, snatched up the cash box for safekeeping, and turned and hightailed it for the small storage area located behind the concession stand.

She pushed inside the small room that housed the concession stand's dry goods, flicked on the light and slumped against the door.

She set the cash box on a nearby shelf, then closed her eyes and drew in a lung full of air that wasn't filled with the intoxicating scent of horse and leather and *him*. There. Now she could breathe again. And think. And remember the all-important fact that while she wanted Houston, she wasn't supposed to want him in front of anyone. That meant no blushing or trembling or kissing.

Especially kissing.

Another deep breath and she opened her eyes. A bare bulb hung overhead, illuminating the small room that housed everything from gallon cans of chili and cheese sauce for the *frito* pies, to five-gallon jars of pickles. Large silver cylinders filled with carbonated soda dominated the far corner of the room. Monstrous bags of corn chips and cases of candy bars lined the metal shelves that ran the length of one wall.

She scooted past several boxes filled with paper plates and napkins and made her way to a six-foot table where she'd left the rest of the goodies the chamber members had donated for tonight's sale. There were dozens of pies and platters of brownies and a few cakes. She was busy reading the masking-tape labels on the tops of the plastic wrap when she heard the door creak open.

"I'll be out of your way in a minute," she called out to whichever concession stand employee had come to retrieve supplies.

"Actually, I'd rather have you in my way." Houston's deep voice slid into her ears and sent a jolt of adrenaline through her. She whirled, bumping the table. Plates clattered and a pie slid dangerously close to the edge.

"What are you doing in here?" She caught the aluminum pie pan a half inch shy of diving over the side.

"I changed my mind." His eyes glittered with a hungry light that sucked the oxygen from her lungs and made her hands tremble. The pie slid from her grasp and tumbled over as she tried to retrieve it before it hit the floor. Crust and filling covered her fingers as she caught the inside rather than the edge.

"You're supposed to be selling those pies, not feeling them up."

"You're really funny." She put down the pie and glanced around for a napkin, but there was nothing except a roll of plastic wrap.

"Actually—" his gaze darkened "—I'm really hungry." He reached for her hand.

Before she could draw her next breath, his tongue flicked out and he licked one finger. Once, twice, before sliding it deep in his mouth and suckling for a breath-stealing moment.

"I..." She swallowed and tried to think of something to say, but with his lips so firm and purposeful around her finger, his tongue rasping her skin, she couldn't seem to find any words. "I—I thought you changed your mind," she managed to say several moments later after he'd licked her hand clean.

"I did."

"But that was peach, not strawberry."

"I didn't change my mind about the flavor. I changed my mind about the pie altogether." He licked his lips, and she had the sudden image of him licking other parts of her body. Lapping at her neck and her nipples and her belly button and the wet heat between her legs.

"I'd rather have the kiss," he continued.

"I'm not selling kisses."

"Even better. While I don't mind paying for one, I never pass anything up that's free."

"That's not what I meant." She licked her lips and instantly regretted the action. His gaze darkened, and pure sin gleamed in his eyes, and she knew he wanted a lot more than just a kiss.

He wanted inside of her, and she wanted him there.

Just not *here,* and certainly not *now.*

The local high school fight song played in the background. The crowd cheered and the announcer's voice came over the P.A. system as the guest team made the kickoff and the game officially started. Even closer, the *pop-pop* of the popcorn maker drifted from the front of the building, along with the hum of the soda fountains and the whir of the cotton candy machine and the noise of the people. There were people just beyond the thin walls of the storage room. People who could walk in at any moment and find good-girl Sarah getting her fingers licked by the town's bad boy.

Her fingers, or other more needy parts of her body.

She stiffened and forced aside the stirring images. "Look, this isn't a good idea."

"What isn't?"

"You and me and, you know, us. We can't do anything here."

"Why not?"

"Because we can't. This is a storage closet, for heaven's sake. It's not even on the list."

"No, but a public rest room is, *public* being the key word. There's a stadium full of people on the other side of these walls."

She shook her head. "It's not on the list."

"It's close enough." He kissed her then, his lips wet and hungry, his tongue greedy as he devoured her.

"I really can't," she breathed, when he finally pulled away. "Not here. There are people—"

"That's the point, Belle. It's a *public* place. We could be discovered any minute. That's the excitement of it. It's all in the risk."

But it wasn't. Her heart pounded at the thought of kissing him, touching him, *feeling* him, regardless of the surroundings. It wasn't her desire to finish the list and fulfill her fantasies about the last four that fed her attraction to him. It was simply him. They could have been anywhere in any situation—alone on a deserted island or smack dab in the middle of the town square during the annual Cadillac Car Cruise—and she would have been just as turned on. As eager. As desperate.

The realization struck just as he tilted his head and touched his lips to hers for another kiss. And then he fingered her nipple through the soft cotton of her shirt and she stopped thinking altogether.

He dropped to his knees in front of her, his hands going to her hips. He paused to knead her bottom through the fitted material of her slacks. Fabric brushed her legs as he slid them down over her thighs, her knees, until they pooled on the floor.

He stood, then slid his hands around to her bottom and lifted her onto the counter. He paused only to grab one of the large wire racks filled with boxes and shove it in front of the door. It wasn't enough to keep anyone out should they want to get in, but it was enough to buy them some time to grab their clothes should they be discovered.

Walking back to her, he wedged himself between her parted thighs. He urged her backward until her back met the tabletop and then he slowly unbuttoned her shirt and unhooked the front clasp of her bra.

He fingered a dollop of strawberry filling from the pie pan. "I really do like strawberries," he murmured before touching the filling to one ripe nipple. He laved the tip, spreading the glaze until it covered her entire areola.

His gaze drilled into hers for a heart-stopping moment before he lowered his dark head. His tongue lapped at the side of her breast.

The licking grew stronger, more purposeful, as he gobbled up the strawberry confection, starting at the outside and working his way toward the center. Sensation rippled up her spine.

The first leisurely rasp of his tongue against her ripe nipple wrung a cry from her throat. Her fingers threaded through his hair as he drew the quivering tip deep into his hot, hungry mouth. He suckled her long and hard and she barely caught the moan that rippled up her throat.

She caught her lip and clamped down as he licked and suckled and nipped. Her skin grew itchy and tight. Pressure started between her legs, heightened by the way he leaned into her, the hard ridge of his erection prominent beneath his jeans. She spread her legs wider and he settled more deeply between them. Grasping her hips, he rocked her. Rubbed her. Up and down and side to side and…

Bam. Bam. Bam.

The knocking barely penetrated the haze of pleasure that gripped her senses. Panic bolted through her and she went still.

"Wait." She grasped his muscled biceps to still his movements.

"You can moan for me, beg for me, scream for me, but otherwise, no talking allowed."

"But someone's coming."

He leaned back, his gaze drilling into hers, so deep and searching, as if he was doing his damnedest to see inside her. "No," he finally said, his fingertip tracing the edge of her panties where elastic met the tender inside of her thigh. "No one's coming,

Belle.'' His finger dipped into the steamy heat beneath. "Not yet.''

One rasping touch of his callused fingertip against her swollen flesh and she arched up off the counter. She caught her bottom lip and stifled a cry.

With a growl, he spread her wide with his thumb and forefinger and touched and rubbed as he dipped his head and drew on her nipple.

It was too much and not enough. She clamped her lips shut and forced her eyes open. But he was there, filling her line of vision, his fierce gaze drilling into hers. Searching and stirring and...*no!*

Her hands trembled and she fought against the pleasure beating at her senses. She stiffened, her hands diving between them to stop the delicious stroke of his fingers.

As if he sensed her sudden resistance, his movements stilled. His chest heaved and his hair tickled her palms. Damp fingertips trailed over her cheek in a tender gesture that warmed her heart almost as much as her body.

"I want to hear you, Belle. I need to.'' His gaze was hot and bright and feverish as he stared down at her, into her. But there was something else, as well. A desperation that eased the panic beating at her senses and sent a rush of determination through her.

Bam. Bam. Bam.

The noise echoed in her head, but it wasn't someone beating on the door this time. It was the frantic beat of her own heart, because she no longer cared if the entire town stood on the outside of the door, waiting and listening.

It wasn't about what everyone else thought about her. It was about him. What *he* thought about her. What *he* felt for her. What *he* wanted from her.

And what she wanted from him.

Reaching down, she tugged at the button of his jeans, pulled his zipper down and freed his hard length. She squeezed him, stroking him from root to tip before sliding her hands around and cupping his buttocks. She massaged him for a moment before working her hand into his front pocket and retrieving a small foil packet. She opened the condom and spread it on his throbbing penis before pulling him closer, until the head pushed just a fraction of an inch inside of her. Pleasure pierced her brain.

She lifted her legs and hooked them around his waist, opening her body even more. He answered her unspoken invitation and with one deep, probing thrust, he filled her.

Her muscles convulsed around him, clutching him as he gripped her bare bottom. He pumped into her, the pressure and the friction so sweet that it took her breath away.

She was vaguely aware of the voices on the other side of the door. But then he touched her nipple and trailed a hand down her stomach, his fingertips making contact with the place where they joined, and all thought faded in a rush of sweet desire. She met his thrusts in a wild rhythm that urged him faster and deeper and...*yes!*

Her lips parted and she screamed at the blinding force of the climax that picked her up and turned her inside out. He buried himself deep inside her one last time and a shudder went through him as he followed her over the edge.

She wrapped her arms around him and held him and, oddly enough, the fact that she would have to walk out of here with Houston Jericho, past whoever beat on the door, didn't bother her now nearly as much as it should have.

The heat, she told herself. It was hot in the storeroom and so she wasn't thinking clearly. Because no way would she want anyone to know that she and Houston had hooked up again.

That would stir gossip and speculation the likes of which Cadillac hadn't seen since Bernice Marshall had come home from the Christian Women's Convention in Austin with a boy toy she'd met and married after partaking of one too many glasses of communion wine.

The very last thing she needed was to tarnish her image. Unfortunately, what she needed and wanted were two very different things, and at the moment, the only thing she really wanted was Houston Jericho.

In her bed and her life.

Temporarily, of course.

9

WHAT HAD STARTED AS A personal visit to Miss Esther's house for a flower consultation had turned into a full-blown landscaping project. Sarah had tried to tell the woman what to plant and where to plant it, but Miss Esther was too old to make such drastic changes to her own yard.

And so Sarah was here now doing it herself. She rolled her palms around the base of the potted hibiscus before turning it on its side and easing the flower and soil from the plastic container. She placed it in the large hole and filled in the area with rich, dark potting soil, packing and smoothing until the plant sat securely in the main flower bed that now spanned the front of Esther Clooney's house.

She repeated the process five more times until she'd filled the area with four-foot-high hibiscus blooms in various colors. The front of the house was perfect for the tropical flower because there were no trees to shade the area. The hot, blazing Texas sun spilled over the lawn, drenching it in light and heat.

She pulled off her gloves and wiped at the sweat

that beaded her forehead, then reached for her bottled water and took a long drink. A drop spilled past her lips and trickled over her chin, down her throat and over her frantic pulse beat.

Her mind went back to Saturday and the storeroom and the way he'd licked her fingers.

It was just a memory, yet her body responded as if he were standing next to her, murmuring into her ear. Her nipples pebbled and her thighs ached and her heart pounded.

That's the way it had been for the past three days since their sixth encounter. It was as if he'd unlocked something inside of her and she couldn't seem to shut it again.

She'd managed after the shower and the movie encounters. She'd slammed and latched the door on her desire and walked away from him.

But he'd walked away from her in the storage room before she'd managed to gather her control and push her guard back into place. She'd had no reason to bolster her defenses, no need to gather her courage and push him away, because he'd pushed away first.

Strictly sex.

She'd obviously gotten her point across to him. He was clear on their objective.

She should have been happy. Relieved. Instead, she felt even more restless than she had before he'd stepped into her shower last week.

More frustrated. More needy.

Because she wanted more from him than the Sexiest Seven.

She shook away the thought. She'd obviously been out in the sun much too long.

Adjusting her hat, she climbed to her feet and spent the next twenty minutes picking up empty soil bags and plastic flowerpots until she'd cleared the area. She tossed everything into the back of her skunk trunk—she'd yet to kill the smell completely—and climbed behind the wheel. Gunning the engine, she shifted the truck into Reverse and backed up to the end of the drive. She needed to get back to the nursery and relieve Arnie. Not to mention, she had a stack of deliveries scheduled for that afternoon and...

The thought faded as her gaze shifted to Miss Esther's yard. She hit the brakes and just sat there.

The newly landscaped yard breathed life into the old gray house. The flower beds added not only color, but a rich, potent vibrancy that complemented the straight, clean lines of the house's frame. The creeping ivy mixed with the white juniper she'd planted in the window boxes flowed over the sides, drawing color and light that reflected off the diamond-shaped glass panes that had been virtually invisible before thanks to the thick window frames and shutters.

She'd always appreciated the clean lines and thick construction of the old farmhouse, but she'd never actually admired the architecture until now. The house was truly beautiful. Even more, it reflected the sweet nature of the old woman who lived inside.

A woman who was now standing on her front porch, a tear sliding down her cheek as she eyed Sarah's handiwork.

Excitement rushed through her, followed by a feeling of pride the likes of which she hadn't felt since she'd opened that letter from the University of Texas architectural college and found out she'd been accepted.

Crazy. These were just flowers and plants and dirt. They weren't a real accomplishment. Anybody could plant flowers and make an old woman smile. And anybody with halfway decent grades could get into architectural school.

But making it all the way through to become a big-time architect...that was something altogether different. It took talent and drive and courage. Even then, there was no guarantee. But that's what had made the notion so appealing in the first place. She'd always liked taking risks and putting herself out there. Sometimes it hadn't paid off, but most of the time it had. She'd been a nerdy schoolkid with no social skills, but she'd wanted to be popular and so she'd put herself out there. She'd been bold and it had paid off. She'd actually managed what most Chem Gems had only dreamed of—she'd crossed over to the land of the popular. She'd ignored the five scholarships that had been offered to her based on her chemistry test scores and had applied to University of Texas. There'd been no scholarship waiting to help her achieve her dream. She'd been ready to work her way through, to make it happen no matter what. She'd been ready to say those three words to the wildest bad boy at Cadillac High School, even though she'd known deep down inside that the odds were against her. She wasn't pretty enough or big-breasted enough or special enough to win Houston's love, if he was even capable of the emotion. But she'd been willing to take the chance.

She'd liked taking chances.

Until Sharon's death.

Until she'd seen her strong, resilient grandmother turn a pale ash and suffer a heart attack right in front of her eyes.

Sarah hadn't realized her own mortality at that moment. She'd realized her Grandma Willie's. The woman was old and frail and Sarah had been pushing her right over the edge with her wild ways.

"Don't ever leave me, Sarah. I need you. I couldn't bear it if something ever took you away from me. Not after losing your mother. I've lost too much already."

Her grandmother's words as the paramedics had loaded her into the ambulance echoed in Sarah's head. She stiffened and shifted into Reverse.

But even as she left the yard and her silly, long-ago dreams behind, she couldn't shake the feeling of pride. It stayed with her as she headed back to the nursery to finish her day.

For the first time, she didn't feel so restless when she sat down in her tiny office at the nursery to check on her new inventory. She didn't feel resentful as she stood out in the hot sun and watered the tropical plants. And when she glanced over at the courthouse across the street, she didn't feel the same sense of oppression she'd always felt. Instead, she felt pride because she'd planted the rows of azalea bushes that lined the winding drive and tapered around toward the sidewalk. Just as she'd planted the lilies that clustered around the base of the sprawling oak trees. And the Texas sage. And the chrysanthemums and the circles of bluebonnets that dotted the sprawling green lawn.

Sarah realized then that while the dream that she nurtured had once been someone else's, it was now her own.

She loved making things beautiful.

Almost as much as she loved Houston Jericho.

Love?

The minute the notion struck, she pushed it aside.

She'd never been the type to fall in love. Back in her wild days, she'd lived for excitement, not the goal of finding her own Prince Charming. While she'd toned down, she hadn't changed her opinion of the emotion—namely, that love wasn't for her. She didn't want to fall in love with someone, to need him, to have yet another reason to sacrifice when she'd already sacrificed so much for the emotion.

For the love of her grandma Willie.

No, she couldn't help but love her grandma. But she could help loving someone else. She could keep herself from falling in love, even with a man like Houston Jericho.

Especially a man like him.

Because he didn't believe in the emotion any more than she did.

"COME ON." HOUSTON GRIPPED her elbow, ushered her outside and steered her toward his truck.

"Where are we going?"

"Time for number seven." His gaze hooked on her for the space of a heartbeat as he loaded her into the passenger's side and her heart kicked up a beat.

"Where are we going?" she asked again when they turned off the main strip through town onto Farm Road 582.

"I told you. Number seven."

"Shouldn't we be at the courthouse or the library?

They're the only two buildings in town with elevators.''

"One's a two-story and the other is three stories. That means five minutes max if we stop between floors. This is going to take longer than five minutes, Belle.''

His words made her heart beat all the faster. They spent the next hour in silence, the tension building around them, between them, the awareness at fever pitch by the time they reached the San Antonio city limits. Lights twinkled and buildings filled the horizon.

After ten minutes darting in and out of traffic in the heart of downtown, Houston pulled into the huge circular drive in front of the River House.

While the hotel might, indeed, be located on the river, it was far from a house. Twenty stories reached toward the sky, the lobby plush with cream-colored carpet and gold fixtures. Houston left her sitting on a sofa near a huge marble fountain while he checked them in. Five minutes later, he led her toward the rear of the hotel that faced the San Antonio River Walk and a row of elevators.

They looked like ordinary elevators with steel doors, but when the doors of one of them slid open, she got the surprise of her life.

The elevators were really glass cubicles located on the outside of the building. They slid up and down the side, giving a full view of the winding river and sparkling lights as they climbed to their destination.

''You can see everything,'' she murmured as they stepped inside and Houston punched the eighteenth floor. Of course, it also meant that anyone who happened to look up could see everything.

The realization sent a zing of arousal through her and her nipples pebbled.

The reaction wasn't lost on him. He fixed his gaze on the soft points that pressed against her T-shirt. He reached out, flicking and rubbing one of the tips through the soft material.

There were no more words as they were whisked to their floor. The doors slid open and he steered her down a hallway to room 1820. He slid the card into the slot, waited for the red light and flipped the handle. Sarah found her small suitcase waiting on the king-size bed, but Houston's bag was nowhere to be found.

''Where's your stuff?''

''In my room.''

''Your room?'' She shook her head as realization hit. ''You booked two rooms?''

''This is about the elevator, not the room. You've been so dead set on sticking to the list, I didn't think number seven would extend past the elevator. Once we're done there, we're done.''

''And we each return to our respective rooms.''

"Exactly." His gaze caught and held hers, and she had the feeling that he was giving her a dose of her own medicine, treating her the way she'd treated him during encounters four and five. She'd shut him out under the pretense that she wanted merely sex from him. Specifically the Sexiest Seven.

You asked for it, you got it.

But she wasn't so sure that she wanted it. Things had changed between them. She'd changed. She'd realized that her hunger for him extended beyond a few fantasies, and she wanted more.

"Relax and get comfortable," he told her. "I'm going to check into my room and then I've got a few things to take care of. We'll get together later."

"Later" happened in exactly fourteen minutes— she had little to do but watch the clock. It was that or dwell on the fact that she truly felt something for him, yet wasn't ready to sort through her emotions right now.

If ever.

Better to anticipate the coming encounter, a feeling that heightened when she heard his deep "Meet me on the top floor" when she answered her ringing phone.

She freshened up, left her hotel room and headed down the hall. After punching the Up button, she waited, her heart pounding as the elevator made a slow descent.

"Going up?" she asked when the doors whisked open and she found him standing inside.

"I'm already up." And then he tugged her inside and into his arms as the doors slid shut and the elevator started humming. They climbed four stories before he punched the Stop button and stalled them between floors.

She stared down at the River Walk below. People filled the outside patios of several nearby restaurants. A boat overflowing with sightseers wound its way down the river. People strolled up and down the sidewalks.

"All anyone has to do is look up and they'll see us," he said, coming up behind her and pinning her to the glass. His hands came around to push up her T-shirt. He flicked her bra open and bared both breasts. "They'll see your pink nipples." He fingered the stiff peaks and she caught her bottom lip. "They'll see me touch them and stroke them." He turned her around and dipped his head. "They'll see me taste them," he murmured before he drew the aching tip deep into his mouth and sucked her so hard that she felt the pull between her legs.

She shuddered as he released her to drag his hot, wet mouth to her other nipple and catch it with his teeth. He flicked her with his tongue, over and over, making her squirm until he opened his lips and suckled her again.

Heat spiraled through her body and pleasure gripped her for several heart-stopping moments. But it wasn't enough. She wanted more. Frantic fingers grappled at his shirt, pulling and tugging until she found her way underneath. Warm, hair-dusted skin met her fingertips and she trembled. Muscles rippled beneath her palms as she trailed them over his chest and down to the waistband of his jeans.

She unbuttoned his jeans with several fierce, frantic tugs. He sprang hot and huge into her hands and she stroked him. Her fingers slid back and forth, tracing the bulging head, the hard, smooth length. She cupped his testicles and massaged them, and his arousal pulsed against her.

He reached for her skirt then, tugging it up to find that she wore no panties.

"All this time?" he asked, his voice raw and pained, as if he wanted her so much it hurt, just as it hurt her.

"All this time."

He turned her and she placed her hands on the glass. His arms came around her and he cupped her sex, dragging a finger over her wet folds in a smooth, sweet rhythm that made her moan.

They stood in full view of anyone who happened to glance up, yet she wasn't the least bit aware. Her senses were focused solely on the man who surrounded her, his hands on her hips, his gaze fixed on her reflection in the glass. Behind her, his arousal throbbed, pressing against her buttocks, hot and desperate for entry.

His palm met the glass next to hers and his other arm slid around her, anchoring her for a full upward thrust until he was buried to the hilt.

He didn't move for a long moment. He just stood there as her body throbbed around his, though they were both standing perfectly still.

She barely heard the ring of the emergency phone through the haze of pleasure that surrounded her. He withdrew then, only to plunge back in. She strained against him, moving her hips and meeting his thrust with a sense of urgency that had little to do with the constant ringing and everything to do with the need building inside her.

He moved in and out in a fierce rhythm. Pleasure splintered her brain with each thrust until she couldn't take any more. She closed her eyes as her orgasm crashed over and consumed her entire body. Tremors racked her and her knees buckled. She went limp, but Houston was there, his strong arms around her, holding her as he plunged deep one more time.

He followed her over the edge, his body rigid as he held himself deep.

She slumped against him and tried to quiet the thunder of her heart. A few seconds ticked by and the ringing suddenly seemed louder, pulling them back to reality much too quickly.

Then again, they'd had more time than if they'd been at the library in town, that was for sure. Dinah Crabtree, the head librarian, would have already called the volunteer fire department for a rescue by now.

"Yeah?" Houston growled as he snatched up the phone. "Yep, my wife was getting sick from the motion of the elevator, so I had to stop it and give her some time to catch her breath." He listened for a moment. "We tried to get off, but the doors stuck on the previous floor and I didn't want her getting full-blown sick. Sorry if it caused any inconvenience."

He stepped away from her and let her skirt fall back into place. He pulled his underwear and jeans back on and hauled the zipper into place. He didn't bother with the button. Instead, he yanked his T-shirt down and punched the On button. With a groan, the elevator started moving again.

Sarah righted her shirt, leaned back against the glass and braced herself as the elevator dropped the three floors to theirs. She stared at Houston's back, wondering how in the world he managed to look so calm and in control after what had just happened between them.

Sex. Uncomplicated, frivolous, meaningless sex.

Yeah, right.

They'd passed uncomplicated, frivolous and meaningless way back when they'd shared their hopes and dreams and those homemade wine coolers.

She'd told him things she'd never told anyone and he'd done the same, and it had forged a deeper level of intimacy than any physical contact. She'd not only fallen for him that night, she'd fallen helplessly in love for the first time in her life.

And the last.

She pushed aside the thought. She would find someone else. Someone appropriate. Someone who would be content with small-town life and a small-town wife. Someone who wouldn't always want more than she could give.

Someone who wanted to build a home and make babies and settle down.

Houston wasn't the man for the job. He couldn't be. He was too busy with his life. Too dead set on keeping his distance and his perspective and staying far, far away from Cadillac and his father's memory. Too hell-bent on being the success on the bull riding circuit his old man hadn't been.

She didn't blame him. She knew what it was like to want something so desperately. Years ago, she'd wanted out of Cadillac, out from under the shadow of her perfect mother, away from the family business. Not because she didn't like the nursery, but because she feared she wouldn't measure up there any more than she'd measured up to her mother's perfect image. She'd fallen short, and rather than risk the same failure with the Green Machine, she'd simply wanted out, to find her own place in the world, find something she was really good at.

She'd already done both, but she'd done them right here.

She'd stopped trying to run the place the way her mother and grandmother had, and started running things her own way. Thanks to Houston. She'd taken on the deliveries and expanded her services to include landscaping, and the business was prospering because of both.

She had her place, all right, and it was right here.

But Houston had found his place somewhere else. Everywhere else. Wherever the next ride took him.

They were different people going different ways.

The doors slid open and he took her hand and walked down the hallway. He unlocked her door, kissed her hungrily on the lips and turned to leave the way he had at the movie theater.

"Wait." She caught his arm and he turned to face her. "Stay here tonight. With me."

While she didn't have a future with him, she did have the next few days, and she intended to make the most of them. When they parted for the second and final time, she didn't want any fantasies haunting her from here on out. She wanted bona fide memories.

"I thought we were finished," he said, but his look told her that he wasn't any readier to call it quits than she was.

"We're not even close." And then she kissed him for all she was worth.

10

THE MOMENT SHE PULLED HIM into a kiss of her own initiative, Houston knew something had changed. There was a boldness about her, an urgency that he'd never seen before.

Actually only once before. When they'd touched for the first time so long ago.

But they'd been kids back then and there'd been an awkwardness about the whole thing that was completely missing now. Instead, they came together on a basic, primitive level that was unlike anything he'd ever experienced before. There was no planning or premeditation involved.

Just pure, wild, uninhibited lust, and something else he couldn't quite name. Something he wasn't ready to name. And both took his breath away as fiercely as the woman herself.

Her mouth ate at his, her touch greedy and hungry, and a groan rumbled from his throat.

She pressed herself against him, her breasts crushed against his chest, her soft curves molded to his hard body so perfectly that he had the fleeting thought that she'd been made for him and only him.

The thought sent a thrill coursing through him, followed by warning bells.

No ties. No commitment. *No.*

He wasn't the man for her. He was temporary, and when it was all over and done with, he would leave the way he always did. Because Houston had been moving for so long, that he wasn't so sure he could stop.

Even if he suddenly wanted to.

His arms tightened around her and he took the lead, the sudden need to brand her with his kiss and his touch more urgent than anything he'd ever felt before. He buried his hands in her hair and tilted her so he could take the kiss deeper. While he was here, he wanted—no, he *needed*—to pleasure her so thoroughly that she'd forget every man in her past except him.

So that when he was gone, she wanted no one but him.

A crazy feeling for a man who made it a point never to feel possessive of any woman. He'd never let himself get that close, never let a female get under his skin and into his head and threaten his priorities.

Except once.

The morning of their graduation when he'd

planned to blow off the ceremony and head down to the creek, and he'd wanted her to go there with him.

The girl she'd been three days prior—before Sharon's death—would have jumped at the chance to thumb her nose at convention. The girl she'd become had merely shaken her head and turned him down.

She'd turned away and then he'd turned away, and they'd both gone their separate ways.

But for those few seconds before they'd parted, he'd read a wealth of emotion in her expressive eyes. She'd even opened her mouth to say the words before she'd thought better of it.

She'd stayed silent and he hadn't pushed her because they'd both known that it had been for the best that she'd kept her mouth shut. Because if she'd said the words, it might have changed everything. He'd been young and foolish and so deprived of emotion his entire life. Hearing the words, seeing them in her eyes, would have been enough to make him stay.

At the moment, the notion didn't seem all that unpleasant. Years of kissing and touching and having hot, wicked sex with the most sultry woman he'd ever met definitely held more appeal than a snorting, smelly bull hell-bent on castrating him.

The sex. He knew it was the excellent, grade-A sex. It was so good that it distracted him and made him think crazy things.

Like maybe, just maybe, hanging around town and taking Miss Marshalyn up on her offer wouldn't be so bad. Maybe he could build himself a little house as bright and as sweet-smelling as the old woman's. Maybe he and Sarah could make a real go of it together. Maybe it would be different for them than it had been for his own parents. Maybe he wouldn't miss the rodeo circuit and come to resent her because she'd been the one to hold him back.

"You're the spitting image of your pa. The spittin' image."

Hank Brister's voice echoed in his head and conjured memories of all the other times he'd heard the exact same thing. The words had challenged him to prove he was different from his pa, and he'd done so. He was nothing like his old man and he never would be, and that's why he would keep moving when the time came, keep riding, and never look back.

But right now... Need gripped him. Fierce. Demanding. Overwhelming.

He kept eating at her lips as he slid his hands down under her bottom and lifted her. She wrapped her legs around him, her naked sex settling over the hard bulge in his jeans. He kicked the door shut and carried her over to the bed.

Once she was settled on the mattress, he followed her. He kissed her roughly, deeply, as he shoved the skirt down her thighs. He worked at her shirt next and then her bra, until she was naked beneath him. And then Houston did what he'd been wanting to do since the moment he'd rolled back into town.

He pleasured her in any and every way he'd ever dreamed of, and he took his own sweet time doing it because this wasn't about fulfilling the list anymore. This was about fulfilling his own need, and he aimed to take all that he could for as long as he could, because he knew it would end all too soon.

In half a week, the day after Miss Marshalyn's party, he would say goodbye to Sarah Buchanan for the second time.

The last time.

THEIR WILD LOVEMAKING in San Antonio ended all too quickly for Sarah. After a long, sleepless night and breakfast in bed, they were on their way back to Cadillac and the real world. Houston dropped her off at the nursery with a rough kiss and a look of promise that told her he would definitely see her later.

She held tight to the excitement swimming inside her and refused to think beyond the next night. And the next. But over the course of the next couple of days, she came to realize that it wasn't just the nights she enjoyed, but the days, as well. Houston showed up each afternoon to help her around the nursery. He moved plants and watered inventory and hoisted the heavy bags of topsoil she'd had delivered from her supplier in Austin. The bags had been selling almost as fast as she ordered them. She even had to dip into the stack she'd set aside for the new landscaping jobs she'd landed, thanks to Esther Clooney's yard.

They not only worked side by side, but they talked, as well. She learned more about his life outside Cadillac and, in turn, she told him about her life here. About how she'd settled down for her grandmother's sake and tried to do right by the old woman. He talked about all the purses and titles he'd won and how he was this close to taking another victory in Las Vegas the week following Miss Marshalyn's party.

He was leaving. Tomorrow. His plane flew out of Austin the day after Miss Marshalyn's party, which was tonight. And Sarah had no doubt that he would be on it.

The truth niggled at her, but she forced it aside, determined to concentrate on the here and now and simply live for the moment. Something she hadn't done in the twelve years since she'd taken herself down the straight and narrow and safe path toward Good Girlsville.

Something she would never do again.

She glanced toward the front of the nursery where Houston was rearranging a row of the new large potted palms she'd ordered for the courthouse landscaping project she'd been offered just yesterday. They were huge and heavy, but he moved them with an ease that sent a burst of admiration through her. And a jolt of excitement.

Muscles flexed and sweat ran down his forearms as he maneuvered the large pots, scooting them this way and shimmying them that way. Her gaze hooked on his hands—large, strong hands that had stroked her to an amazing climax near the crack of dawn the other morning when he'd rolled over her and into her, waking her from her sleepy haze in the most pleasurable of ways.

The door chimed, the sound jerking her from the memory, and she turned to see Imogene Asbury walk inside. The young woman glanced around as if looking for someone. Sarah killed the spray and was about to call out when large hands caught her shoulders from behind and steered her around.

"Hide me." Houston's deep voice echoed in her ears.

"What are you doing?" She tried to turn, but he kept her directly in front of him.

"I don't want her to see me."

"Who?"

"Imogene. She's here for me."

"How do you know?"

"Because she's been following me around since Cheryl Louise's wedding. It seems Miss Marshalyn told her hairdresser, who told her friend, who told Imogene's mother that I wanted to take her out. Since then, she's been following me around, trying to make a date. Just get rid of her, would you?''

''Get in the back storeroom and I'll see what I can do.''

Sarah gave Houston time to take cover before she pasted on her best smile and picked her way past rows of plants toward Imogene.

''Have you seen Houston Jericho? Mrs. Morgan over at the bed-and-breakfast said her husband had told her that his friend's wife had spotted him here the other day.''

''You just missed him.''

''Darn it. I really need to talk to him. See, there's this date,'' she started, before shaking her head. ''Never mind. If you see him, could you just tell him that I'm looking for him? Here's my number.''

Once the bell had chimed again and the door had closed, Houston walked out of the storeroom. ''That was close.''

''Here you go.'' She handed over the paper. She watched him glance at it before stuffing it into his pocket. An image rushed at her. Of Houston talking and laughing with Imogene, and a pang of jealousy went through her.

She stiffened and frowned, the emotion extremely

unsettling to a woman who'd made up her mind to feel only lust for the man in front of her.

Her grip on the water hose tightened.

"Thanks. That was close. She almost caught me yesterday. I barely made it out of the diner without attracting her attention."

"How long have you been avoiding her?"

"Since Miss Marshalyn put out the word that I'd come back home to settle down and find a wife."

"But you're not the least bit interested in settling down or finding a wife."

"You're telling me."

"So why don't you just set the record straight? Just tell her you don't want a date."

"I couldn't do that. She might cry. I don't do crying women—hey!" he sputtered as she turned her hose on him and gave him a good squirt in the face. "What was that for?"

For making me feel so possessive and jealous and threatened.

"For leading that poor girl on."

"I'm not leading anyone on. I never told her I would go out with her."

"You never told her you wouldn't."

"I haven't talked to her since the sixth grade, and that was just to ask her to switch desks with me so that I could get away from Carol Ann Busbee, who kept blowing kisses at me every time I looked at her.''

"You should go after her and straighten this out right now."

He fixed his gaze on her for a long moment as if he was trying to figure something out. Then his lips curved into a grin. "If I didn't know better, I'd say you were jealous."

"I am not jealous. I'm practical. Hiding is just plain ridiculous."

"I don't know. I sort of liked ducking down behind you. The view was pretty good."

Her heart kicked up a notch and she turned the hose on him again for a quick spurt.

"Hey, stop that. You're getting me all wet."

As if she hadn't noticed. His white T-shirt, now practically transparent, stuck to him like a second skin, revealing every bulge of muscle, every ripple of smooth sinewy flesh as he reached up and wiped a hand over his wet face.

"You deserve to get soaked. That poor girl obviously likes you. You should go after her and set the record straight."

"I'd rather stay right here and enjoy the view. You look good wet."

"I'm not wet."

"Not yet." Before she could draw her next breath, he snatched the water-hose nozzle from her hands and waved it threateningly. "If memory serves me, you not only look good wet. You look good soapy, as well."

His last words conjured images from their shower encounter, when she'd been covered with nothing but slick soap and water and him.

But this was different, she reminded herself as her ears tuned to the sound of a passing car. They weren't in the privacy of her house or hidden away in a storage closet or off in the next town in some dark movie theater or in a fancy hotel hours away.

They were right here in a public place, in the bright light of day, where any of the fine, upstanding citizens of Cadillac could happen upon them at any time.

Twelve years of pretending, of hiding, kicked in and stirred her panic, because Sarah Buchanan truly had morphed into the good girl she'd spent so much time pretending to be.

"We don't have any soap," he continued, "but I guess I could settle for one out of two."

"Don't even think about squirting me," she told him, despite the thrill that rushed through her. She frowned. "I mean it."

The devil danced in his gaze as he eyed her. "What will you give me if I don't squirt you?"

"What do you want?"

"You."

"That could be arranged."

"Right here, right now. Naked."

"Later, in the bed—" she started, the words fading in a sputter as water rushed at her face in a quick spurt. She wiped at her face and cracked an eye open to see him smiling at her.

"Wrong answer," he told her. "Now, let's try it again. I want you right here, right now. Naked."

"But someone could walk in—" Another burst of water came at her, this one aimed at her chest. The liquid turned her pale pink T-shirt nearly transparent, her lace bra clearly visible beneath. Her nipples pebbled, poking through the lace pattern to press against the material.

"Wrong answer, Belle," he said again, his voice drawing her gaze. He wasn't smiling at her. Instead, his eyes had darkened into a smoldering look that told her he was done with the teasing. "That's the point. Anyone could come in and then they would know what we've been doing this past week. Would that be so terrible?" When she didn't answer, disappointment flashed in his gaze, as if he were hurt that she wanted to keep their relationship a secret. As if he wanted the world to know that she was his and he was hers.

As if.

It was a foolish notion, yet she couldn't help the surge of warmth that went through her, followed by the desperate urge to erase the hurt from his expression. She licked her lips, and the simple act seemed to heighten his arousal.

"I want you," he said again, his voice rougher, pained even. "Right here, right now."

"You forgot naked." The light in his gaze fed the desire inside of her until she wanted him so much that she forgot everything except the need inside her.

She grasped the edge of her T-shirt. The wet material slid up her abdomen and the undersides of her breasts before catching on her fully erect nipples. Excitement blossomed, making her pulse quicken and her body ache.

"I'm stuck," she murmured, as if it were some terrible dilemma that she couldn't quite solve. In truth, she wanted to turn him on so fiercely that he felt the same emotion that suddenly raged inside her.

She tugged this way and that, the material rubbing a delicious friction against the ripe tips. A few more delicious seconds and she managed to pull the material up and over her head. Her fingers went to the front clasp of her bra. The fastening strained then snapped open and the cups fell away. She unfastened her khaki slacks and pushed the soggy material down her legs. With her fingers hooked around the straps of her panties, she shoved them all the way down and stepped free. "How's this for an answer?"

His answer was a muttered curse that burned her

ears as much as his gaze burned every inch of exposed flesh. He closed the distance between them and claimed her lips in a deep, thorough kiss that told her he wanted her as much as she wanted him.

She expected him to sweep her up into his arms, but he didn't. Instead, he left her standing there to walk to the front of the nursery, flip the lock and turn the Out to Lunch sign. A few strides and he was back, and he was kissing her.

His lips ate at hers, his hands slicking over her wet skin as if he couldn't feel her thoroughly enough. His sudden frenzy fed her own and she clawed at his T-shirt, desperate to get underneath. Her fingertips met warm flesh and she groaned. She tugged at his waistband, pulling the button free and shoving the zipper down until she touched his hard, thick penis. His solid length pulsed in her hand and raw hunger rushed through her.

She dropped to her knees and took him into her mouth. She suckled and laved, relishing his sharp intake of breath. The sound filled her with a burst of confidence that made her want him all the more. She wanted to taste him and savor him, but he had other ideas.

''I need to be inside you.'' He hauled her up into his arms and steered her around until he'd pinned her to the wall. He lifted her and plunged deep inside before she could draw her next breath. He was so strong and powerful as he filled her, surrounded her, consumed her. She breathed in his scent, soaked up his body heat, drank in the sound of his harsh panting, but it wasn't enough.

She had to see him, and she opened her eyes to find him staring at her, into her, seeing her for who she really was and wanting her in spite of it. Because of it.

''I love you.'' The words spilled past her lips before she had a chance to remind herself that the last thing she wanted to feel for Houston Jericho was love.

He went stock still, and she had the sinking feeling that she'd made a big, big mistake. But then he slid his arms around her and held her tight and she forgot everything except the next fierce thrust of his body. She shattered in his arms and he quickly followed, spilling himself deep inside.

Neither of them said anything for the next few frantic moments as he held her, and she clung to him and their hearts thundered. All too soon, however, he eased her to her feet and she opened her eyes to reality.

To…love?

Surely she hadn't said something so totally ridiculous and inappropriate and… Oh, God, she'd said it.

Worse, she *felt* it.

The thought sent a swell of happiness, followed by a rush of dread, because she didn't want to love him. He was wild and free and on the move, and she was settled right here. There was no point in loving him. It was useless and crazy.

That was it. She'd been so sexually frustrated after walking the straight and narrow for so long that when she finally happened into some really great sex, the excitement had blown several major brain cells. She didn't love him. She couldn't love him. She *wouldn't* love him.

"I... You... We..." She shook her head. "I didn't mean it," she blurted as she bent to retrieve her clothes. "I mean, I meant it. I love the way you make me feel, but I don't love you." She tried for a laugh, but it came out sounding rusty and forced. "I don't." She said the words more for herself than him. "I really don't."

"But—"

"It was the heat of the moment, but now it's not nearly so hot."

"It feels pretty hot to me and that sounded pretty real."

"It was just lust. People mistake lust for love all the time. Not that I'm making that mistake. I mean, I did just a few moments ago, but I'm not perpetuating it. I know the difference."

"You do, huh?"

''And this isn't even close.'' Truthfully, it was too close. And he was too close. And it was getting increasingly harder to keep her distance. As it was, she had the insane urge to touch the pulse beat at the base of his neck just to see if his blood still rushed as fast as hers. ''Lust,'' she said again. ''So don't worry that I'll make more of it. And don't worry about forgetting the condom because I'm on the pill.''

The words seemed to send a jolt of reality through him as if he'd just remembered his desperation to be inside her and the all-important fact that he'd forgotten the damned condom. The look quickly faded into a frown. ''Why are you on the pill? I would think that living like a nun wouldn't call for birth control.''

''You never know.'' Truthfully, it kept her regular, but she wouldn't tell him that because it didn't sound nearly as exciting and while she'd accepted that she was a bona fide good girl for the most part, she hadn't admitted the truth to him. ''I've been waiting to cut loose for so long and I wanted to be prepared. It's a good thing I was because we both got a little crazy. I mean, you without the condom and me saying such a ludicrous thing.''

The strange thing was, he didn't look any more convinced than she felt. Instead, he looked…angry.

As if he didn't want her to try to explain away the slip. As if he wanted...

She was definitely crazy. Why, he didn't want her love any more than she wanted to give it to him. He'd said it many times.

"Settling down isn't for me. I want to go places and do things and live. I don't want to be tied to this hellhole of a town for the rest of my life like my old man. Now, that would be hell."

Even so, he eyed her for a long moment and she couldn't help the feeling that he wasn't just searching for the truth, but he actually wanted to find it.

"Boy, it's getting late," she blurted, eager for something to fill the awkward silence. "Don't you have to get ready for Miss Marshalyn's party?"

His expression faded and he glanced at his watch. "I did promise my brother that I'd help set up tables for the party tonight."

"You can't be late for that. I mean, that's what these past two weeks have all been about, right? Sticking around for the party?"

"Yeah," he said, but his gaze said something altogether different. That there was more. That he felt more.

Maybe. Maybe not. Either way, it didn't matter because it didn't change the truth—he was leaving and she was staying right here. And she wasn't going to put off the inevitable for one more night in his arms.

She'd managed to regain her perspective after they'd made love this time—namely that she shouldn't love him, and she didn't, and their relationship was only temporary—but she wasn't so sure she could do it a second time. If she touched him again, loved him again, she feared she'd say the dreaded words all over again. More important, she feared she'd feel them deep in her bones, and act on them by asking him to stay.

She wouldn't put herself on the line when she already knew his answer.

"You'd better get going. Be careful," she told him once he'd fastened his jeans and reached into his pocket for his keys. "And take care of yourself."

"How dangerous can setting up tables be?"

"I'm not talking about the tables. I'm talking about Vegas, and everything after."

Before he could say a word, she stepped toward him and touched her mouth to his. She wrapped her arms around him as if she never meant to let go. She gave him everything in a fierce, blazing-hot kiss that intensified the longing deep inside her and made her want to hold him for the rest of her life.

But then she did what she knew she had to do. She pulled back and let him walk away.

And then she cried.

11

HOUSTON NURSED HIS BEER and forced his gaze away from the entrance to the Knights of Columbus Hall, where everyone in town had turned out to tell Miss Marshalyn goodbye and wish her well.

Almost everyone.

The party had started more than two hours ago and Sarah still hadn't shown up. Not that he'd expected her to. She'd made their goodbye clear that afternoon after she'd said those three little words that he'd purposely avoided his entire life.

A declaration that didn't bother him nearly as much as it should have. No, what sat in his craw was her poor explanation and the fact that she'd felt the need to give one. She obviously didn't want to feel anything for him.

Thankfully. He didn't want her to feel anything. He didn't want any ties. Nothing that might harness him to Cadillac when he fully intended to ride away come tomorrow morning.

Tomorrow. That's what he needed to focus on. He had a championship ride waiting for him. A record-breaking moment. The chance to go down in the history books as not only a winner, but *the* winner. The only consecutive ten-time champion in the history of the sport.

The prospect didn't excite him nearly as much as it should have. Instead, he felt…disappointed.

And annoyed. Damned annoyed.

"I don't know what the hell I'm doing." Austin Jericho's voice drew him around.

Houston turned to see his older brother looking as bad as he felt. He didn't seem to have shaved for a couple of days, and he looked tired. Worn. Worried.

"What's up with you?"

"You don't want to know," Austin said. When Houston gave him a questioning glance, he just shook his head and wiped his face, as if trying to erase the lines. "I brought Debbie the Kindergarten Teacher tonight."

Houston's gaze went to the petite redhead standing near the punch bowl. She smiled, the picture of grace and perfection as she handed out punch cups. "She looks nice."

"She is. That's the problem. She's too nice." He shook his head. "That's not what I mean. She's nice, but it's not the right kind of nice. She's not the right woman."

"So why did you bring her?" Austin gave him an as-if-you-don't-know look. "Miss Marshalyn will see right through it. She always saw right through everything. Like the time you stole that bushel of peas to use in your shooter and she asked you about it."

The reminder eased the lines around his older brother's eyes and drew a smile. "She was this close to tearing a strip off me."

"But you gave up the bushel before she found her switch. You were always coming clean with her. That's why I have to admit, I'm a little surprised. You must want that land pretty bad."

"I do, but not half as much as I want…" The words trailed off as a thought seemed to strike him.

"Debbie?" Houston arched an eyebrow.

"Maddie."

"I thought her name was Debbie."

"*Her* name is Debbie." Austin pointed to the punch-bowl woman. "The woman I want is Maddie Hale." He glanced around. "I've got to set the record straight." Just as he turned, he pinned Houston with a glance. "You should do the same."

"What's that supposed to mean?"

"You should have brought Sarah tonight. You like her. You've always liked her."

"I don't like her." *Like* was too mild a word for the feelings whirling inside him. He felt attracted to her, drawn to her, mesmerized by her.

"You like her, all right. You ought to tell her."

"You ought to practice what you preach instead of prancing in here with a woman you have no interest in."

"I might be interested."

"And I might sprout wings and fly right out of here."

"Okay, so I'm not interested. I'm stupid. That doesn't mean you have to make the same mistake. Tell Sarah how you feel."

"If I felt anything, it would only make things harder. I've got a bull with my name on it."

"So tell her and take her with you."

As if she would go. She had her business and her grandmother. She would never leave the old woman and risk upsetting her. She would stay right here and keep living her lie.

And you'll head on out of town and keep living yours.

A lie? He wasn't living a lie. He was living his dreams, doing what his father hadn't had the courage to do.

Or maybe he was the courageous one for staying and facing his responsibilities, while you're just running away.

Houston pushed aside the crazy thought. His old man had been many things, but courageous wasn't one of them. He'd stayed in Cadillac, but he sure as shootin' hadn't faced his responsibilities. He'd run from them, straight into a bottle where he could mourn the loss of his dreams and blame anyone and everyone but himself. He'd been a coward.

"Tell her," Austin pressed, drawing Houston's attention away from his damning thoughts.

"We're not kids anymore. I don't need you telling me what to do."

"Actually, you need a boot up your backside for being so damned stubborn."

"Says who?"

"Says me."

"As if you could do it."

"I guess you forgot that time when I shoved your head under the bed and made you cry uncle because you drove the lawn mower over Miss Marshalyn's prize-winning bluebonnets."

"I thought they were weeds. Hell, they grow everywhere around here. How was I supposed to know they were some hoity-toity breed?" A grin tugged at his lips. "You really kicked my ass good back then."

"You needed it."

"And you always were the first to point it out. You've always been a good brother, Austin. You were the reason Dallas and I made it. You were there for us."

"We're family. You, me, Dallas and Miss Marshalyn."

"That's why you're here with the kindergarten

teacher, isn't it? It's not about the land. You didn't want to let Miss Marshalyn down.''

He nodded. ''But I suppose she'll be even more let down when she realizes that there's nothing to it.''

''*If* she realizes it.''

''She'll realize it, all right, when I tell her the truth.'' He pinned Houston with a stare. ''You ought to do the same.''

''I have nothing to hide from Miss Marshalyn. I always speak the truth. It's my downfall. But she doesn't want to hear what I have to say. I don't want her land.''

''I'm not talking about Miss Marshalyn. What about Sarah?''

''What about her?''

''You care about her.''

''What if I do? It doesn't change anything.''

''Maybe it would. Maybe she'll pick up and go with you.''

''She won't do that, and I wouldn't ask her to, any more than she would ask me to stay.'' She wouldn't. She didn't want to face her feelings, much less take a chance and ask him to stay.

Because he wouldn't. She knew it. He knew it. It was simply a fact of life.

Austin shook his head. ''As stubborn as ever.''

Houston grinned and quickly changed the subject.
"I learned from the best, bro."

Austin shrugged. "I never knew being stubborn
could be so damned lonely." He clapped Houston on
the back. "If I don't see you before you take off,
call me when you get to Vegas." At Houston's nod,
he turned and walked off toward Miss Marshalyn.

You like her.

Austin had it all wrong. Houston didn't like Sarah.
He'd passed "like" a long time ago. What he felt
was much stronger, more intense.

Frightening. Or it should have been. The fact that
it didn't bother him half as much as it should have
was damned disturbing in itself. Because Houston
didn't want to feel anything for anybody.

No ties. No regrets. No reason to stay.

He took another sip of his beer and his heartbeat
kicked up when the door opened. He watched as
Imogene Asbury walked in with a woman who
looked like an older version of herself. Probably her
mother and the other half of the matchmaking team
of Myrtle and Miss Marshalyn.

He remembered Sarah's words about "leading the
poor girl on," which kept him from running for
cover. He'd never considered avoiding someone the
same thing as leading them on, but maybe Sarah was
right.

Oddly enough, it wasn't the *maybe* that urged him

to his feet. It was the image of Sarah, her eyes alight with jealousy and something that looked suspiciously like hurt, that motivated him to set his beer aside and make his way through the crowd. It wasn't a matter of hurting Miss Marshalyn's feelings. It was all about setting the record straight and reassuring everybody else in town, including one doubtful Sarah, that he had no designs on Imogene Asbury.

"Can I talk to you?" he asked when he reached her.

Her head snapped up from the plate of goodies she'd picked up. "It's you. Why, I've been looking everywhere for you."

"I know. That's what we need to talk about. About this date we're supposed to have—"

"I can't," she interrupted. "I mean, I can. I'm single and everything and so a date is a possibility. But while I'm still single, I'm not really single. I'm in love and so a date really isn't possible. I can't do that to him."

"You're in love? But your mother said you were looking for someone."

"She hates Melvin. He has big ears and he never says thank you and she has issues with that. But I love him and he loves me. I really hate to disappoint you."

"Disappoint me? I mean, yeah, this disappoints me, all right." He put on his best wounded expression and she smiled. "But I suppose I can get over it."

"I do hope you find someone."

Her words stuck in his head, along with Sarah's image, and he headed back to the bar for another beer.

Three beers and he still felt as stone-cold sober as before. And every bit as miserable. How his father could have ever found any answers in a bottle was completely beyond Houston. Alcohol didn't numb the pain. It magnified it.

"I saw you talking to Imogene." Miss Marshalyn's voice drew him around just as he waved away beer number four and reached for a glass of ice water. He turned to find her standing next to Spur Tucker.

"She's already spoken for."

"Melvin hasn't even given her a ring."

"She loves him, anyway, and that's what counts."

"Since when?"

Since Sarah Buchanan had blurted out her feelings in the heat of the moment and made him the happiest man alive.

He forced aside the notion. "She loves him and she's not going out with anyone else, least of all me. So you can forget trying to hook me up."

"I swear, you men are the most clueless creatures on the face of the earth."

"What's that supposed to mean?"

"That it's not about 'hooking you up' with anyone. It's about knowing in my heart that you're happy."

"I am. I'm damned happy." Or he had been earlier that afternoon for those few moments when Sarah had said those three words to him. Until reality had set in and he'd remembered that he didn't want her to love him, any more than he wanted to love her. He wasn't doing the settling down, domestic thing. He liked being on the road and living out of a suitcase and being successful.

"I worry about you."

"I'm all grown up."

"I know that. It's just been hard to accept. But you are, indeed, a grown man now. A good man."

"I'm not a rancher." He eyed his brother, who stood across the room, far away from the fresh-faced kindergarten teacher. "But I know somebody who is."

"You don't have to sell me on your brother. I know he's good at what he does, and I know he deserves his share. He's already told me how he tried to pull a fast one and I'm sure that he suspects that I'm not going to give him a blessed thing."

"He can't help the way he feels."

"Any more than you can help the way you feel." He knew she saw the surprise on his face. "I know you truly don't want the land. You're not a rancher. You're a big, bad bull rider and you've got better things to do than mess with a bunch of old cows.''

''I like cows. But I like bulls better.''

''You like dishing up the bull*shit*.'' At his sharp glance, she added, ''What? A woman can't tell it like it is once in a while?''

''What would the senior ladies down at the beauty shop say?''

''I don't care what they say. It's taken me a while to admit that, but I truly don't. I care about the people in my life. I want you and your brothers to be all right when I'm gone.'' She shook her head. ''Your brother shouldn't have tried to fool me tonight.''

''He loves you. He wanted to make you happy. We all do. I was tempted to bring someone tonight, myself.'' But after what had happened today, he hadn't been able to bring himself to pick up the phone and call Imogene. ''Not for the land, mind you. For you. I don't give a rat's rump about those hundred acres. Not that I don't appreciate your offer,'' he added, his voice softening. ''I do. I appreciate everything you've ever done for me and my brothers. You were always there for us.''

''Sweetie, you boys were always there for me.''

He grinned. ''We were always pestering you.''

''True, but I wouldn't have had it any other way.

You three came along, always needing your noses wiped and your stomachs filled and your fannies swatted. You were a pain in the butt, but you made my life full.''

His lips curved in a full-blown smile as he remembered a particular episode from the past when she'd chased him out of her strawberry patch with a three-foot switch.

''You gave us a real home when we didn't have one of our own. I wish I could repay you for that, but I can't. Not like this. I can't give up everything I've worked so hard for just to come back here.''

He'd been living on the road, anticipating the next ride for so long that he didn't know if he could give it up.

Even if he suddenly wanted to more than he wanted to draw his next breath.

''I'm not asking you to give up anything. All I ever wanted was to know that you were okay. That you were happy. That I didn't have to worry over you anymore.''

''Like I said, I'm all grown up now.''

''I know that, and I'm proud of you. Still a little worried, of course. I'm entitled to my opinion, and as far as I'm concerned it's crazy to climb on top of a thousand-pound animal who wants nothing more than to stomp you to bits.''

''It's exciting.''

"Maybe, but it's still crazy. But if that's what you want, then you're entitled to it."

"That's what I want," he said, but the words didn't hold as much conviction as they usually did.

"That's your choice. You're all grown up, and you just proved it."

"How's that?"

"You didn't compromise your dreams for someone else. That shows that you're not the same little boy who was always stealing cookies from my cookie jar to take home to a hateful old man who never appreciated them."

"Maybe I ate those cookies."

"And maybe *Playboy* is beating down my door for a centerfold shot."

He let loose a low whistle. "I always knew you were hot to trot."

She frowned. "You were always trying to coax a smile or a kind word out of your father. You wanted his love, and so you compromised your own time and effort to try to please him, just the way your father compromised his rodeo dreams to marry your mother. I was always afraid for you, fearful that you would do the same thing."

"I'm not my old man."

"No, you're not. You've got your hopes and dreams and you're not willing to compromise them for anyone. That shows maturity. I didn't want to see that. I was so focused on you getting hurt. I wanted you here. Settled. Safe. But that's not for you, whether I like it or not. At least you had the courage to stand up for yourself. You didn't buckle just to please me.'' She patted his arm. ''And you don't owe me for anything. You and your brothers gave me a purpose in life when I desperately needed one.'' She kissed his cheek. ''In truth, I'm the one who owes you, and now I'm paying up.'' She handed him an envelope. ''I want you to know I'm giving Austin your land because he learned how to tell the truth himself and honesty should always be rewarded. But mainly he's getting it because I know he'll put it to good use while you're tending your own place.''

''Actually, I haven't seen my apartment in a couple of months.'' He turned over the envelope and opened it. ''I go straight to Vegas tomorrow for a few practice rides before the preliminaries start this weekend.''

''You'll have to get someone to feed the dog, then. And water the roses. I'll not have them drying up while you're gone. Why, I'll never be able to focus on my new life and my new eyesight if I have to worry about dried-up roses.''

''I don't have a dog.'' He pulled a legal document from the envelope. ''And I sure as shootin' don't have any roses.''

''Of course you do.'' She patted his arm as he

unfolded the paper. "And you've got azalea bushes, too. And creeping ivy. And lilies. And lots of pure-bred bluebonnets that somehow managed to survive a vicious lawn-mowing incident some years back."

"What are you…" His words trailed off as he stared at the name listed on the top. "This is the deed to your house."

"It's the deed to *your* house," she said, and then she turned to walk away. "You don't have to make a living here. Just take care of it and come back every now and then."

"But…" he started, but she simply waved and started walking, leaving him to face the enormity of what had just happened.

He stared down at the deed of trust. Joy erupted inside him for the second time that day, stirring another wave of panic that made his heart pound faster and his feet itch to move.

Shoving the deed into his back pocket, he headed for the rear exit. Home or no home, Houston Jericho wouldn't stay in Cadillac. He couldn't. He wasn't going to live out his life in this desperately small town. No matter how appealing the idea, or how much he enjoyed giving pointers out at Hank's place, or how much Sarah Buchanan loved him.

He was holding on to his goals, his dreams, his

pride, and following them straight out of town. Something his father hadn't had the courage to do.

So why did it suddenly feel as if he was leaving behind things that mattered most?

The question haunted him as he gunned the engine and headed through town. Before he knew what he was doing, he'd turned onto Sarah's street. Her house sat to the right, the porch light blazing. He slowed and braked to a stop and simply sat there. Thinking. Looking.

The front drapes were parted, the sheers trembling with the small breeze. They did little to hinder the view, however. He could see her sitting on her sofa in her oversize pajamas, a bowl of popcorn on her lap, the television set blazing. He had half a mind to march inside, strip off the ugly old pajamas, haul her into his arms and simply hold her.

A need that had nothing to do with sex and everything to do with the fact that Sarah had lived and breathed in his memories for so long that he couldn't seem to forget her. He knew that they could go through the list, repeating scenario after scenario, and it would never be enough to get her out from under his skin and out of his heart.

Because somehow, some way, despite his best efforts, she'd found her way inside for good.

His fingers tightened on the steering wheel as he forced the notion aside and stepped on the gas. A few minutes later, he walked into his room at the bed-and-breakfast and started to pack, because no way, no how was he giving up his entire life to stay in this dead-end town just because he'd fallen in love.

Because Houston Jericho wasn't going to make the same mistake his father had made.

IT WAS BARELY TEN O'CLOCK the next morning when Sarah rang up an order of potted petunias and wheeled the purchase out to Mr. Montgomery's car. She loaded the plants into the back of his station wagon and waved goodbye before walking back inside, past a six-foot-high stack of potting soil bags still sitting in the exact spot that the delivery driver had unloaded them into first thing that morning.

It had been three hours since she'd unlocked the doors and opened for business, and Houston still hadn't shown up.

She didn't expect him to after what she'd said yesterday. It was enough to spook any man, particularly one who'd made it perfectly clear that the last thing he wanted, the *very* last thing he wanted, was love or marriage or anything that might interfere with his life on the road.

Even so, a small part of her had held out hope that he would come riding up, declare his love, and they would live happily ever after the way that couple had done in the old black-and-white movie she'd watched on the late, late show last night.

She'd closed her eyes and settled back on the couch and pictured him charging through the door, hauling her into his arms and telling her that she didn't have to feel afraid or disappointed or regretful because he loved her, too, and he wanted to be with her.

But those had been silly dreams.

This was reality. Her nursery. Her responsibility. Her life. And it was right here, while his existed hundreds of miles away. Not that the distance was the real problem. The real problem was that he simply didn't return her feelings because Houston Jericho didn't believe in love.

He believed in sating his hunger and satisfying his baser needs. Lust, pure and simple.

That's what she told herself.

But lust didn't explain why he'd lost his control yesterday and forgotten all about the precious condoms he always wore. He'd been madly, desperately in lust since he'd walked back into her life, yet not once before had he been so overwhelmed he'd forgotten a condom.

It was almost as if he'd wanted a deeper commitment from her. More of a reason to give it all up and stay right here. She had no doubt that he would never abandon his child. He would step up and do the right thing and stand by her.

But she didn't want Houston Jericho and his sense of duty. She didn't want anything from him.

At least that's what she told herself as she went about her morning and tried to ignore the painful truth.

Houston Jericho was leaving.

Again.

HE WAS LEAVING, ALL RIGHT. You're damned straight he was.

He'd told himself that all night as he'd sat down by Cadillac Creek and watched the sun come up. He'd thought of every reason why he should leave, why he wanted to leave, but it still wasn't enough to make him drive past the county line, toward Austin and the plane that waited for him, and his life beyond his hometown.

He got close. But every time he started to pass the Y'all Come Back, Now, Ya Hear? sign, he would remember some barn where he'd thrown rocks or some house that he'd always admired, and he would have to turn around, eager for one more glimpse of his past, dead certain that one more look would be enough to ease the turmoil raging inside him and close that chapter of his life once and for all.

He'd driven down every dirt road and followed up

on every small memory, but nothing eased the ache in his chest. He'd run out of places to go and things to see and there was nothing left but the small road that turned toward the cemetery where his father had been buried so many years earlier during that record-setting cold day in February.

Not that he'd felt the cold firsthand. He'd been far away in Cheyenne. Too busy winning to slow down for anyone or anything, least of all his father. It wasn't as if the old man would have wanted him there, anyway. He'd never wanted Houston or his three brothers, any more than he'd wanted their mother when she'd been alive.

Even so, the three boys had been a constant presence in his life, always picking him up when he passed out or urging him to eat to counter the effects of the alcohol, yet he'd hated them, anyway. He'd resented them. He'd abandoned them.

The only reason Houston had felt even a small measure of guilt was because his brothers had had to deal with the arrangements without him. But it was Austin and Dallas who'd convinced him to stay in the finals in the first place. They'd wanted him to win, to make a name for himself. To make a name on the outside that would be celebrated rather than frowned upon the way it was right here in Cadillac, thanks to their drunk of a father.

No, Houston sure as hell didn't owe the old man anything. Not then and not now.

But he owed himself.

Sarah was right. The whole funeral thing wasn't so much for the person in the casket, but the people all around it. To give them an opportunity to come to grips with their loss.

And maybe, just maybe, if he took the walk down that path and saw for himself that the old man was truly dead and buried, gone for good, somehow he could shut out the voices once and for all.

He glanced at the plane ticket sitting on the dash. He didn't have time for this. If he left now, he could just make it.

Even as he told himself that, he reached for the door handle and climbed out of the truck. He lifted the latch on the gate and started down the long, winding track.

His chest tightened with each step, until the air sawed past his lips and his heart pounded a fast, furious rhythm.

A few steps and he rounded the twin oak trees into a small clearing. He blinked and stared at the freshly planted flowers that surrounded the simple headstone. The weeds had been pulled, the grass mowed. New shrubs circled the area. His heart revved as his gaze touched a cluster of bright yellow daisies. *Sarah.*

He thought back to that day in the truck when they'd made their first nursery delivery and she'd commented on the lack of flowers at his gravesite.

"He didn't deserve flowers."

She'd said both the flowers and the funeral were for the people left behind. They were a way to say goodbye.

He'd told her he didn't need to say goodbye. That's what he wanted to believe. Because if he needed closure it would mean that his dad's thoughts and opinions had actually mattered to him. That Houston had actually liked the old man. That maybe he'd even loved him, despite that his father had never returned that love. Well, no way. Not for all the cookies in Miss Marshalyn's cookie jar.

Bick Jericho hadn't deserved anyone's love. And he hadn't wanted it, as he'd said many times, fortifying the wall between himself and his three sons. As though if he made it thick enough and high enough, he wouldn't have to worry about feeling anything for them. And he wouldn't have to worry about losing them the way he'd lost his wife.

That's what Houston told himself. What he knew to be a cold, hard fact. At the same time, he couldn't help but remember that first time his father had taken him to Hank Brister's and set him on top of that mechanical bull. And the way he'd plopped Houston on his shoulders that one Christmas morning and bounced him around. And the way he'd kissed Houston's mother on that last and final visit they'd made to the hospital before her kidneys had given out for good.

Those were the only good memories. Too few to count, he told himself.

But they did count.

They were burned into his memory and he couldn't forget them. Even more, he couldn't hate his father the way he wanted to. The way he should, considering the old man had been bitter and jealous toward him.

"Go on and get out of here. You won't make it. You'll be back here just like me. Stuck here, just like me."

He'd been ready to come back to prove his old man wrong, but it had been too late. There'd been no convincing the man that despite the uncanny resemblance, Houston was nothing like him. Houston was a winner, not a loser. Not a drunk, no-good loser who didn't have balls big enough to step up and be a man and take care of his boys. And love them the way they'd wanted to be loved.

The way Houston still wanted to be loved.

Bick hadn't had any tolerance for such an emotion. *"Love'll cripple you, boy. You mark my words."*

But it wasn't love that had turned his father into a bad husband and an even worse father. Houston realized that as he stood there amid the daisies and the bluebonnets. It was love that had turned this neglected spot into a beautiful landscaped garden.

It was fear that had been his father's downfall. His father hadn't given up his dreams because he'd been saddled with a wife and kids and he'd had no other choice. He still could have fulfilled his dreams had he been courageous enough to pursue them. No, he'd been afraid to try and even more afraid to fail. And so he'd run from that fear, straight into a bottle.

When the truth hit Houston he closed his eyes. He'd spent all these years convincing himself that he was nothing like his old man, yet he was just like him.

In appearance and in deed.

His father had run straight into a bottle to escape his fear of failure as a prize-winning bull rider, just the way Houston had run away to escape his fear of turning into the same bitter man his father had once been. As though if he stayed far, far away from Cadillac and commitment and anything that even resembled permanency, he could save himself from the same fate. But by leaving, he'd done just what his father had done for all those years.

Well, no more.

He truly wasn't his old man, because he didn't hate the thought of spending the rest of his days right here in his hometown. He loved the notion and, more important, he loved Sarah Buchanan.

She just didn't know it.

Yet.

12

———

"I'LL HAVE THE ROSE BUSHES planted first thing next Wednesday," Sarah told Jake MacIntyre from the mercantile. He had a planter in front of the store that he'd wanted to fill with poppies. She'd talked him into roses since he was trying to draw in more of a female clientele to try the new cosmetics counter he'd added at the back of the store.

"Now, you're sure they'll smell good? Maybe we should go with jasmine. I've got some jasmine perfume and it ain't too bad."

"Jasmine doesn't do well in full sunlight. The roses will do much better during the summer months. We'll keep them thriving in the colder months with a portable ground heater that keeps the soil warm and comfortable. So you'll be good to go all year round."

"I do like red roses. Pick 'em up for my wife every Valentine's Day."

"Now you can pick her a stem or two for no special reason. I bet she'd like that."

"She'd probably ask me to stick out my tongue for fear I'm running a fever. I'm not the romantic sort. No candy or wishy-washy cards. Just the flowers once a year.''

''For most women, it's the little things that count. Like when a man buys an entire fudge cake just to get a chance to talk to a woman, or when he buys a box of Sugar Babies at the movies because he remembers how much she likes them. Or when he weeds her flower bed because she doesn't have the time.''

''Uh, yeah.'' He gave her a funny look.

''Not that any man has ever done that for me. I don't have a man in my life.'' Funny how the words didn't come as easily as she expected, considering that she'd already come to terms with the fact that Houston Jericho was gone.

She wanted him gone. She had an image to maintain and they'd reached the end of the list.

And she loved him.

She forced the notion aside. It didn't matter if she loved him. Love didn't change anything. It didn't make them different people. She still had her life and he had his.

And more important, he didn't love her back.

Not that she wanted him to.

At least that's what she told herself.

She showed him the bill. ''Here you go. Here's everything, including the delivery charge.'' He finished signing his check, handed it over and took his receipt. "See you on Wednesday."

Sarah left the counter and headed down an aisle of large potted crepe myrtle plants. She needed to work. To concentrate on caring for the massive inventory she'd built over the past few weeks for the new landscaping services she was now offering.

She'd just grabbed her scissors and started to prune a few dried leaves when she heard the bell ring.

Her heart kicked up a notch as she glanced around a branch.

Jake MacIntyre waved at her. "Could you do it Tuesday? I'd really like to have the planter filled by then."

"Will do. I'll change the job on my schedule and be there in the afternoon."

"Perfect."

No sooner had the door shut than he pushed it back open again. "How about Monday?"

"My day is full." He frowned and she added, "But I could schedule it for the late afternoon."

"Perfect." The door closed.

She'd just turned back to the crepe myrtle when the doorbell trembled and tinkled again.

"I don't work on Sundays," she called out.

"I hope not, because I had something much more

relaxing in mind.'' The deep, familiar voice slid into her ears and brought her around.

She turned to find Houston standing in the doorway looking so tall and handsome and real. Her heart revved and her hands trembled.

''I was thinking that you might stop by my place for supper.''

''What are you doing here?''

''I had to see you.''

''Don't. I hate long goodbyes and—''

''This isn't about goodbye. It's about saying thank you.''

''What are you talking about?''

''My father's grave. You were out there. You did it for me. Because you do love me.''

''You're wrong—''

''I *know* that you love me.'' He touched a hand to his heart. ''I know it right here. I feel it. I felt it the day before yesterday, but then you made that crazy excuse and I believed it because I wanted to believe it. Because I was scared. I've been running from my own feelings for so long that my gut instinct was to bolt, to accept your explanation and get the hell out so that I didn't have to accept the truth. You do love me. You really do love me.''

''I…'' She shook her head. ''What brought you back?''

"I ran because you said you loved me, and I came back because of it. Because I want to hear it again."

She thought about denying him, but the sudden desperation in his gaze had her saying the words before she could stop herself. "I love you." There. It was out and she wasn't taking it back. She tried to concentrate on pulling off her gloves. "Not that it changes anything. I know that you're leaving and I won't try to stop—"

"I love you."

"—you and I certainly won't break down and cry and— What did you say?"

"I love you. I've always loved you. From the first moment we drove down to the creek and watched the sun set, until now. You made me so crazy with your enthusiasm for everything. You liked standing on the edge and peering over the side. You liked the rush that comes from really living."

Joy rushed through her, a feeling that quickly faded in a wash of despair. "It still doesn't change anything. You're not staying and I'm not going." She met his gaze. "I'm not. I thought about it. About picking up and just going after you because I can't live without you. But the thing is, I live here and I'll always live here. I like my life. I always have— I just didn't realize it. I was so set on preserving the girl I'd once been, on reclaiming her just as soon as I had the chance, but she's changed. She's all grown up. She's me. Conservative. Tame. Small-town. And you're not. You never will be. And you'll never be content with someone who is."

"You're not tame, Belle." He touched her then, his fingertip gliding along the slope of her jaw, under her chin to tilt up her face. "You're just scared because of Sharon's death. Because it could just as easily have been you."

"I'm not afraid to die."

"No, you're afraid to live. Afraid to take a chance, afraid to get hurt. Afraid to risk the safe little world you've created for yourself."

"You don't know what you're talking about."

"I know you. You're afraid, all right. I saw it in your eyes yesterday when you told me that you loved me."

"You saw no such thing."

"I saw everything. I always have."

"I am *not* afraid."

"Trust me," he continued, despite her denial. "Fear can't keep you warm at night, and it sure as hell can't make you happy. But I can." He kissed her then in a hard, rough way that left her lips tingling when he pulled away. "I can make you happy because I know who you really are. Your wild streak didn't fade. It's in there, hiding behind the fear. That's the difference now. You're scared, but you don't have to be. You can let go the way you used to. Trust yourself, Sarah. You won't make the same mistakes. And neither will I. I'm not leaving again. Not this town. Not my home. Not you. Not ever." And then he turned and walked away.

IT TOOK ALL OF HOUSTON'S control to keep from folding her over his shoulder, taking her down to the creek and reminding her of their past and proving to her that he'd loved her even then.

He had, he just hadn't realized it until now.

She had to come to her own realization, and when she did, he would be right here in Cadillac. Ready and waiting for her.

In the meantime, he had to see a man about a bull.

He climbed into his truck and drove out to Hank's place. He found Harley in the barn rubbing down a worn-looking mare.

"Where's your dad?" he asked the young man.

"He's over at the feed store picking up grain for the cattle. You here to ride the bull?" Excitement lit his gaze, as usual when old Nell was mentioned. It was a feeling Houston knew all too well because he'd felt it most of his life.

"Actually, I'm here for something altogether different. But speaking of riding, why don't you climb on up and I'll work the controls?"

"I couldn't. I've never been on a bull before. I'll eat dust the first few seconds."

"Probably, but then you get back up and climb back on and you ride again. And each time you do it, your time will get longer."

"You think so?"

"I know so. You've got the fever. I can see it in your eyes. And it's the fever that guarantees a successful ride. There are bull riders the world over who are skilled, but they don't want it bad enough. If you want it bad enough, you're halfway there when it comes to a successful ride. The rest is simply a matter of practice and technique."

"I guess I could try." Harley set aside his grooming tools and entered the corral while Houston headed into the tack room, flipped the switch and returned to the control panel. The young man climbed up and Houston opened up the bull to half throttle.

"Cowboy up," he called out, and then he gripped the toggle and gave Harley his first taste of bull riding.

Sure enough, the younger man lasted only two seconds, but eating dust didn't deter him. He grinned, his juices pumped after the exciting ride, and climbed back on.

Harley was on his eleventh try and up to three seconds when Hank rolled into the barn.

"What's going on here?" Hank's gaze went from Harley to Houston.

The excitement drained from the young man's face when his gaze fixed on his father.

"Just conducting a little test." Houston left the control panel and walked toward his old mentor.

"What sort of test?"

"A test for this new business I have in mind."

"A business?"

"A rodeo college. Right here at your place. You and me. I put up the capital and you supervise the operation, and between the two of us we'll turn this old barn into a state-of-the-art training facility for rodeo cowboys. We'll be the instructors."

"Who are we going to instruct?"

"We'll start with your boy there. He's got a steady grip and I think he's a natural."

Hank's gaze shifted to his son. "You really rode old Nellie?"

"I…" Harley licked his lips. "I'm sorry, Dad."

"Sorry?" Hank's face broke into a smile. "Why, that's great, son."

"Great? But I thought you wanted me to be a veterinarian."

"I thought you wanted to be a veterinarian. You applied to the program."

"I only did that because you kept saying I had a way with animals and I should use it."

"There are lots of ways to use that talent."

"But I didn't think you meant bull riding. You're

always saying you want more for me than an endless string of rodeos and a world of hurt.''

''I meant that I want you to do better than I did. If you want to rodeo, more power to you. But do it better than me. Be smarter than me. If that's what you truly want. That *is* what you want, I take it, judging by that silly grin spreading across your face.''

At Harley's nod, Hank turned to Houston. ''Then I guess we've got our first student and you've got yourself a deal.''

Houston shook the older man's hand. He had a deal, all right, but what he didn't have was the one thing he wanted most in his life.

He didn't have Sarah.

And as stubborn as she was, as determined to ignore her feelings for him as she was to ignore his feelings for her, he worried that he never would.

He loved her, but for the first time he started to think that maybe, just maybe, it wouldn't be enough.

HE *LOVED* HER?

He couldn't. More important, he wouldn't, Sarah told herself throughout the rest of the day.

Houston wasn't the type of man to fall in love with any woman. He was the catch-ya-later kind, too busy with his bull riding career and his determination to prove his old man wrong to waste his time with such an emotion.

And even if he did love her, he didn't love *her*.

He'd fallen head over heels for the girl she'd once been. Wild and spontaneous and oblivious to everyone and everything but her own needs and desires.

She cared about people now, and she cared about this town. This was her present, her future, while it was merely his past. He lived for bigger and better places. For the next moment and the next ride.

I'm not leaving again.

Maybe so, but it wasn't because he'd fallen for her. Maybe that last bull had kicked him in the head as well as the ribs.

That was the only explanation for his declaration, not to mention his ridiculous claim that she was scared of living.

Why, she wasn't scared of anything except hurting her grandmother. Which was why she made it a point to be early for their weekly dinner that night. And extra cheerful. The old woman meant too much to her, and Sarah would never put her on an emotional roller coaster the way she had back then. She didn't want her grandmother worried or upset or sad.

"I'm worried, dear," her grandmother told her when Sarah slid into the seat opposite her. "You don't look so good."

"I feel fine."

"I don't mean sick. You look…unhappy. Is something wrong?"

"What could possibly be wrong? Business is good. The landscaping is really taking off." Sarah noted her grandmother's pale complexion and panic rushed through her. "You look tired, Grandma Willie. Did you get enough sleep last night?"

"Of course I did."

"I think you should take a nap. Right after dinner, we'll go into the living room and I'll tuck you in on the couch."

"I really don't want a nap."

"I'll even rub your feet the way you like."

"Well, maybe I could…" Her words trailed off as she shook her head. "No, I'm through letting you fuss over me, even if you do give the best foot rubs in town. This isn't about me. It's about you. Things aren't going well for you." She pinned Sarah with a knowing stare. "You're having trouble in your personal life, aren't you?"

"Of course not. I'm fine. Great. I mean, as good as can be expected considering I don't really have much of a personal life. I'm focused on the business. Totally and completely focused."

"That's terrible."

"It is?"

"And a complete load of bunk."

"What do you mean?"

"That Melba Calhoun from my domino group had dinner with the mayor's wife's mother, who told her that the police chief's wife saw you with Houston Jericho."

"She did? I mean, yes, I suppose she did. He sort of helped me out with my deliveries at first. But that's over and done with. He's leaving town."

"That's a shame."

"Not that our business association could really be considered personal— That's a what?"

"A shame. He's a handsome boy."

"His last name is Jericho."

"So?"

"As in the wild Jericho brothers. As in every mother and grandmother's worst nightmare."

"That was a long time ago, dear. He seems to have grown into a fine young man. His brothers, too."

"But you forbade me to see him way back then."

"He wasn't so fine back then, but he was young. We all make mistakes when we're young." She waved a forkful of brussels sprouts at Sarah. "Speaking of youth, I hope you realize that yours is fading fast."

"What's that supposed to mean?"

"That you need to get out more. Have some fun. Otherwise, you're going to wind up an old maid."

"You want me to *date?*"

"I want you to be happy, dear. And you're obviously not happy now." Her face grew serious. "You haven't been for a very long time. I've seen it, but I didn't want to see it. I wanted you to be happy here with me. I wanted to believe you liked giving me foot rubs as much as I liked receiving foot rubs."

"I'm more than happy to give you a foot rub."

"You're a dear, sweet child. But truthfully, you're not happy here with just me, and you shouldn't be. You need people your own age. You need to live life. You need to fall in love." She eyed Sarah's plain Jane outfit. "You need to lighten up. You're much too pretty to be dressing like an old woman."

"Grandma Willie, I don't understand any of this. I thought you liked me like this."

"I did. Or maybe I just liked the idea that you weren't out getting into trouble." A smile touched her lips. "You did have a hankering for that."

"I was wild and reckless and totally unreliable."

"You were young and full of life. Just like your mother."

"I was— What did you say?"

"That you're like your mother. You are, you know. Now, and back then. She had a rebellious streak, too. She was just a lot better at hiding it from me. That's how she met your father. She snuck out one night to go to a party—I'd forbidden her to go because I thought she was too young—and she danced with him and it was love from then on."

"You never told me that."

"I didn't tell you a lot of things because I feared losing you the way I lost her. To your father, and then to the Lord himself when they both passed on. So I focused on all of her positive attributes, trying to give you a good role model to follow. I wanted to mold you into all of the good things your mother had been, and weed out the bad. And I succeeded, didn't I?" She gave a sad shake of her head. "But in the process, I sucked the life right out of you." She slid her hand across the table and touched Sarah's. "I don't like you like this. You used to be so happy. You used to be so alive. Even when you were facing off with me, there was this vitality about you. But now..." She gave Sarah a direct look. "You need to get a life, dear. Find yourself again. Get in touch with the old Sarah."

The words should have sent a rush of euphoria through her. She'd longed her entire adult life to hear her grandmother say such a thing to her. To free her.

But the truth was, the girl she'd been was gone. What had started out as an act to convince everyone else had turned into a real transformation.

She was content with her life the way that it was. She wasn't scared to live life, as Houston had said.

He was totally and completely crazy.

HE WAS TOTALLY AND completely right.

Sarah admitted the truth to herself later that night

as she watched the videotape of their kiss at the wedding reception. Even then she'd been holding back, despite that she'd initiated the kiss.

She'd pulled back first, startled and shaken by the intensity of one measly kiss.

The truth was right there in the bright glitter of her eyes, in the nervous tremble of her hands, in the startled expression on her face.

She'd told herself she'd been fearful of watchful eyes. But truthfully she'd been fearful of the emotion he stirred. The want. The need. The *love*.

Because she was scared of taking a chance and falling all over again for a man she couldn't possibly have a future with. He'd been her first love, and he'd broken her heart when he'd left town to pursue his dreams while she'd settled for her self-made prison right here in Cadillac, and so she'd vowed that he would be her last love. She'd shut herself off to any and every man after that, afraid to lose her heart and feel the same pain. Her good-girl image facilitated her fear. She'd been able to turn down dates and avoid relationships on the pretense that she'd turned into a wholesome girl who was saving it all for the man of her dreams.

But she hadn't been saving it all for the man of her dreams. She'd been saving herself for a living, breathing man who also happened to be the man of her fantasies.

A man who was now very real and right here, and completely in love with the woman she used to be.

That's what she wanted to think, but she couldn't forget the way he grinned whenever she blushed, or looked so satisfied when she trembled in his arms, or the way he'd laughed when she'd tugged her hem down in the truck during their first delivery. He liked the good girl by his side as much as he liked the wild woman in his bed.

And she *was* still a wild woman, despite that she also had a safe, conservative side. She was both.

She realized that as she replayed in her mind the kiss at the wedding reception and again felt desire clear to her bones. It wasn't the sex that had made her uncomfortable with Houston, but the way he'd looked at her during such a vulnerable moment that had frightened her. Because he hadn't just looked at her. He'd looked *into* her.

She'd been afraid for him to see her feelings, afraid to feel such feelings, and even more afraid to act on them.

Afraid to take a chance and put herself out there. To trust her instincts that told her he did, indeed, love her as much as she loved him. Because if she'd trusted her gut so long ago, she would have been crushed in the passenger seat that fateful night with Sharon.

"We all make mistakes when we're young."

Her grandmother's words replayed in her head.

Young. Not wild. Or irresponsible. Or untrustworthy.

But she wasn't a kid anymore. She was a grown woman. And she was in love. And she knew just how to prove it.

"COWBOY UP!" HOUSTON signaled Hank, who sat behind a large control panel. The older man threw a switch and old Nell roared to life.

The mechanical monster jerked this way and reared that way and the young man holding tight to the cinch strap stayed on for the space of two heartbeats before flying through the air and landing smack dab on his back.

"That was good, Eli," Houston said as he walked over and extended a hand to the young man from a nearby ranch who'd turned out for the first official Bull Riding 101 class given at the Double H Ranch— Hank's place had been renamed to reflect Hank and Houston's new partnership.

It had only been two weeks since Houston had made his proposition and put up the capital to renovate the large barn, but already word had spread like wildfire. They now had twelve wannabe rodeo stars perched on the corral fences, eagerly awaiting the chance to ride old Nell beneath Houston's watchful, professional eye and become the next PBR champion. Not to mention Houston had a stack of applications in his office awaiting placement on a waiting list for the next semester.

The young men, and even one young woman, came from all backgrounds throughout the county. A few were hired hands from nearby ranches, one was the grandson of Ben Skeeter, who owned the pharmacy. There were a few farmers in the mix, as well as the local senior track star from the high school. There were a few seasoned cowboys who'd been rodeoing for years now but had never worked up their courage to move on to the main event. And there was the town pediatrician, who'd always nursed fantasies of being the next Houston Jericho or Bucky Johnson, but had never had the chance to turn his dream into a reality. Until the Double H Ranch had opened up shop.

Houston had forfeited Vegas and his tenth championship in favor of moving into Miss Marshalyn's place. Oddly enough, settling into the old house that had been his only real home as a child felt better than any eight seconds he'd ever spent on top of a foaming, mad bull. The house gave him the sense of acceptance he'd searched for most of his life.

There was only one thing that still kept him tossing and turning at night. Only one thing he truly wanted but couldn't have.

"I tried to hold my form like you said—" Eli started, before his gaze snagged on something and he turned.

Houston followed his gaze toward the barn doorway. As if his thoughts had conjured her, Sarah stood there staring back at him. His heart stalled in his chest for a long moment as two important things registered.

She was, indeed, here. And she looked different.

It wasn't just that she wore a pair of jeans and a fitted tank top rather than her usual conservative, drab slacks and long skirts that clued him in to the change. It was the determined light in her eyes as she walked toward him, the intensity burning bright, fully visible to anyone who might glance at her face.

The mask was gone and she was simply Sarah. As sexy as ever. As headstrong as she'd always been. And she didn't seem to care who saw her.

She headed straight for him, past the curious gazes and toward the corral, her familiar red cowboy boots quickly eating up the distance between them.

With each step she drew closer, into the corral and straight up to where he stood with Eli.

"What happened to you?"

"I wanted you to know that I haven't changed. I mean, I have. I don't really feel one-hundred-percent comfortable in all of this—it's been a long time—but there are moments when this is who I still am.''

"I don't understand.''

"I'm still a bad girl, but I have good-girl tendencies now. I have changed. I'm both now. But one thing hasn't changed. I love you,'' she blurted, despite the curious gazes trained on her. "I always have and I always will and I just didn't have the courage to tell you. Then when I did find the courage, the time wasn't right because I didn't have this.'' She wiggled a small box free from her jeans pocket. "I had to order it and it just came in today.''

"What's going on?'' He felt blindsided.

Without so much as a glance at the surrounding group of people, she dropped to her knees and stared up at him. "Houston Jericho, will you marry me?''

"You're proposing to me,'' he said vaguely as he focused on the box she opened and saw the gold twisted band nestled on a bed of velvet. "*You're* proposing to *me*.''

"I wanted you to know that I'm not afraid to take chances. I'm not afraid to put myself out there. I'm not afraid to live. The only thing I am afraid of is living without you.''

Joy rushed through him, followed by a whirlwind of emotions that gripped him so intensely, the only thing he could do was pull her to her feet and into his arms and hold her so tight he knew he had to be cutting off her circulation.

But he couldn't help himself. He was afraid to let her go and find out that this moment was merely an extension of the fantasies he'd been having every night. Hot, heated dreams that didn't just have her warming his bed, but his heart, as well.

"Is that a yes?" she murmured into his shoulder.

"Not quite." He set her back then because he had a proposition of his own to make. "Not yet."

"You're turning me down?" Her eyes went dull.

"I'm taking my turn, Belle." And then he pulled out the small box he'd been carrying for the past couple of weeks, since the day at her shop when he'd declared his feelings for her. "I wanted to ask you a long time ago, but I didn't think you were ready. But you're ready now." He dropped to one knee, took her hand and stared up into her eyes. "Will *you* marry *me?*"

"Yes." Her full lips curved into a smile that warmed his heart as much as her nearness warmed his body. She let him slip the ring on her trembling finger. *"Yes."*

And then he pushed to his feet, drew her into his arms and kissed her. And Houston Jericho knew the instant their lips met that he'd finally come home.

HARLEQUIN® *Blaze*™

Look for more

Men to do!

...before you say "I do."

#126 TAKE ME TWICE
Isabel Sharpe (March 2004)

&

#134 THE ONE WHO GOT AWAY
Jo Leigh (May 2004)

*Enjoy the latest sexual escapades
in the hottest miniseries.*

Only from Blaze

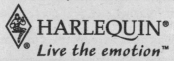

HARLEQUIN®
Live the emotion™

Visit us at www.eHarlequin.com

HBMTD2

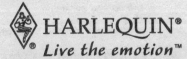